Operation Clean Sweep

Also by Darleen Bailey Beard

The Babbs Switch Story
A novel

The Flimflam Man
A chapter book with pictures by Eileen Christelow

Twister
A picture book illustrated by Nancy Carpenter

Operation Clean Sweep

Darleen Bailey Beard

Farrar Straus Giroux / New York

The characters in this book are purely fictional. Any resemblance to actual people, living or dead, is entirely coincidental.

Distributed in Canada by Douglas & McIntyre Ltd.
Printed in the United States of America
Designed by Jay Colvin
First edition, 2004
7 9 10 8 6

www.fsgkidsbooks.com

Library of Congress Cataloging-in-Publication Data
Beard, Darleen Bailey.
Operation Clean Sweep / Darleen Bailey Beard.— 1st ed.
p. cm.
Summary: In 1916, just four years after getting the right to vote, the women of Umatilla, Oregon, band together to throw the mayor and other city officials out of office, replacing them with women.
ISBN-13: 978-0-374-38034-2
ISBN-10: 0-374-38034-1
[1. Women—Suffrage—Fiction. 2. Elections—Fiction. 3. Umatilla (Or.)—Fiction. 4. Oregon—History—1859- —Fiction.] I. Title.

PZ7.B374Op 2004
[Fic]—dc22

2003049430

This book is dedicated
to the women suffragists who fought
for over seventy-five years for the right to vote.
Many died before the Nineteenth Amendment
was added to the United States Constitution,
granting all women the right to vote.
May we all be as tenacious
in standing up for our beliefs.
May we all pursue our dreams
and cherish the journey.

ACKNOWLEDGMENTS

I would like to thank the kind people of Umatilla, Oregon, for being so generous with their time, photographs, and memories of this historic event in the early days of Umatilla: Canda Rattray and her husband, Alan Curtis, who opened up their home to me and helped me find the historical documentation I was searching for; Alva Stephens; Erma and Smiley Ostrom; Mary Sherrow; Sam Nobles, who came home early from an out-of-state trip just so he could offer his assistance on this book; Margaret D'Estrella; Umatilla Chamber of Commerce; Umatilla Museum & Historical Society; Umatilla City Hall; McNary Heights Elementary; Marie Baldo of the Umatilla Public Library; and George Hash, mayor of Umatilla.

I am grateful to Bob Kingston, reference librarian at the Oregon Historical Society Library; Karen Bratton, research librarian at the Douglas County Museum of History & Natural History; Kathy Finley and the staff at the City of Yoncalla; Clem Deward, curator of the Pioneer Indian Museum in Canyonville; Peggy Madden, library media specialist, who came up with the title for this book; Julie Jarnagin, my former assistant; Patti Binger of

Webgrrl Designs, who keeps my Web site up-to-date and full of energy; and the reference staff in the children's department and the information services department at the Norman Public Library in my hometown. Thanks, also, to the dedicated teachers, library media specialists and coordinators, and principals whom I've met on my many author visits to schools all over the United States. And special thanks to my son, Spencer, for sharing his fishing expertise with me for this book. Thank you all!

Operation Clean Sweep

One

"STICKY STRIKES AGAIN

"November 29, 1916—Sticky Fingers Fred, the most notorious pickpocket in the West, struck the unsuspecting town of Arlington last night, cleaning the pockets of innocent people who attended the annual Arlington Winter Festival.

"Without being seen or heard, this canny criminal confiscated jewelry, watches, and money, including an antique necklace worth over two hundred dollars.

" 'Amazing!' declared a shook-up Mrs. Deetle, owner of the necklace. 'It was around my neck one minute and gone the next!' "

I stopped reading and put my hand around my neck. How could anyone be so smooth as to take a necklace off a lady's neck and her not even feel it?

"Go on, keep reading," Dad said.

Otis took his spring-loaded, nickel-plated tape measure from his pocket and extended it about two feet to make it tap me on the shoulder. "Yeah, keep reading," he said.

"Sticky, whose real name remains unknown, can be identified by a large scar on his left cheek. He stands five feet six inches tall, with a slim build and brown hair. He is known to be a master of disguise, having posed as a priest, cowboy, train conductor, Boy Scout leader, and even a secret agent.

"This makes the tenth town hit in the last eight months. It appears this evildoer is headed east through Oregon, preying on large gatherings of people.

"Citizens are urged to be on the lookout for this seedy character. Police say he may be armed and dangerous. There is a $500.00 reward for anyone with information leading to his capture."

I put the newspaper down on the desk in Dad's office and stared at my best friend, Otis Gill, then at Dad. "Gee, can you believe this dirty dishrag?"

"Oh man!" Otis's eyes lit up. "Wish he'd come to *our* town!"

"Yeah!" I agreed. "Then we could catch him and get the reward money!"

Dad ran his knuckles across the tops of our heads. "Wait a minute, you two. He may be armed and dangerous. Remember that."

I took a swig from my pop bottle. "Do you think he'll show up at our election day parade next week? It's a large gathering of people. That's what the newspaper says he likes."

Dad nodded. "Cornelius, I think you're right. I wouldn't be too surprised if he did show up."

"Gee! I've never seen a real live pickpocket before," Otis said. "I wonder what he looks like. You think he has beady eyes?"

"I *know* he has beady eyes." I pulled Otis's arm and led him to my dad's bulletin board, which was covered with WANTED posters from all over Oregon and even Washington State. "See?" I pointed to the one that said: WANTED—STICKY FINGERS FRED—DEAD OR ALIVE.

"Gee willikers!" Otis said. "Look at those eyes!"

The photo showed a dark-haired man dressed in a checkered shirt. He had a scar going from his left eye all the way down to his lips. His eyes were beady, all right, the beadiest I'd ever seen.

"It says that he took the cuff links off a dead man," I said, reading the small print. "Can you imagine? Stealing the cuff links off a *dead* man?"

"That gives me the creeps," Otis said. He measured the poster. "Hmm, let's see, now. Eight and one-half inches by eleven inches."

"Oatmeal? Do you have to go around measuring *everything*?" He'd been driving me crazy ever since his uncle gave him that tape measure a couple of months ago. At first it was sorta fun, going around measuring things and tapping people with it, but lately it was getting on my nerves.

"No, I don't have to, Corncob. I just want to." Otis put the tape measure back in his pocket and turned toward my dad. "So you really think he's headed this way?"

"There's a good chance he could be. Since we don't know for sure, I'm going to post men at both entrances to Umatilla on the day of the parade. If that bum shows up, we'll throw him in the clink before he even has a chance to blink. That'll make me look good in front of Lanier, won't it?" Dad laughed at his own joke.

Next Tuesday was our election day. Kim Lanier and Dad were both running for mayor. Dad was already mayor, hoping for a second term. Mr. Lanier happened to be Dad's longtime archenemy. In a strange kind of way, they seemed to enjoy making each other miserable. Dad said Lanier was a mud-slinging dingbat who didn't know the first thing about politics. And Lanier said Dad was a slimy scalawag, and that *he* didn't know the first thing about politics. It wasn't a pretty sight.

I didn't tell Dad this, but in a way, I kinda hoped Dad wouldn't be reelected. Back when Dad wasn't mayor, when he worked at the roundhouse, where the train engines got on turntables and changed directions, he had lots more time for fishing, hanging out, and even whistling. He used to be the best whistler around. He and I would whistle duets in church, and we always got lots of compliments. Sometimes we even got invited to whistle at weddings, but we didn't care too much about that because weddings always made ladies cry, and crying ladies made us nervous. I mean, how do you whistle a whole song and keep a straight face with a bunch of weeping, sniffling women in the audience?

Sheriff Vinson walked into Dad's office with a pile of papers under his arm. "Here's that report you requested, Frank." Then he noticed us boys. "Are you two looking forward to the parade? It's going to be a big one this year. We've got all sorts of automobiles and tractors and horses."

"Sure are," I said.

Otis and I loved the election day parade. And why

shouldn't we? Not only did we see and eat lots of stuff, but we got out of school for one whole glorious day. That was about as good as it got. Not that we didn't like school or anything, it was just fun to take a break now and then.

Mr. McGrath, our teacher, was the best. He kept us posted on a daily basis about the Great War, going on over in Europe. Every day he brought in the newspaper and shared it with us, telling us the latest happenings—who was gaining ground, who wasn't, where the troops were, and all the details, even the juicy, gory parts. I knew from him that the United States was almost certain to join the war in 1917, which was only a month away. And I knew that millions and millions of men had already been killed, and that there didn't seem to be any end to the fighting.

"You boys anxious to hear who gets to blow the bugle to commence the parade?" Sheriff Vinson asked. He put the pile of papers down on Dad's desk and exchanged it for another batch.

"Yeah! Who's it gonna be?" I asked.

Otis smiled extra big. "I got to do it last election," he said. "Remember?"

Remember? How could I *not* remember? That was all Otis talked about two years ago. I was sure hoping that this time I'd be the lucky one, but I wasn't holding my breath. There were lots of boys in Umatilla and all of them wanted to blow the bugle.

"Well, I can't say just yet who the lucky boy is," Sheriff Vinson said, winking at Dad. "But don't worry. You'll find out soon enough." He tossed us each a lemon drop, then headed out the door.

"Say, boys," Dad said, "I've got a meeting with the council in about five minutes. Did you two need anything?"

"Nope. We were just stopping by on our way home from school," I told Dad. I dug down into my pocket and pulled up the pocket watch that he had given me for my twelfth birthday. It was the same one his dad had given him on *his* twelfth birthday. I ran my fingers over the embossed largemouth bass on its gold case and took a look at the time.

"Three-forty! Otis, we've got five minutes to get to my house or our moms are gonna scalp us alive!"

Otis and I hightailed it down the board sidewalk, past Mahoney's Drug Store, where they made the best chocolate sodas in town, and along Main Street. We landed at my house just in time for our mothers' weekly card game. Somehow, we had been roped into watching the little kids for these gatherings. We didn't mind too much, though, because of all the good food that the ladies brought.

"Cornelius Thorton Sanwick!" Mom said. "It's about time!"

Sparky, my Australian shepherd, bolted through the doorway, almost knocking Mom off her feet. Sparky jumped up on me, looking me in the eye, licking my face.

"Hello, Dirl!" I said. Dirl was Sparky's nickname. It started out as *Girl*, but through the years evolved into *Dirl*. I made her get down.

"Shake? Shake?"

Sparky held out her paw.

"Good Dirl!" I rubbed her ears. "Sneeze, Dirl. Sneeze."

Sparky sneezed.

"Good Dirl!"

"Let me try," Otis said. "Roll over! Roll over!"

Sparky didn't seem to mind the "S" tricks—shaking, speaking, sneezing, sitting. She even went along with "come" and "heel." Sometimes. But rolling over seemed to be too much effort unless she saw a treat in our hands.

"Roll over!" Otis insisted.

Sparky sniffed Otis's hands, then mine. When she realized they were empty, she lay down with a thud.

"Boys, wipe your feet and come on in," Mom said.

We scraped the chicken poop from the bottom of our shoes. We were used to that. There weren't any rules about chickens in Umatilla, so folks let them run wild in town. Mom and her friends were constantly complaining because their long petticoats and skirts dragged on the ground, working like chicken poop scoops.

We boys didn't care for it much, either. Especially in the summertime, when we walked around barefoot. Having ooey-gooey chicken poop squish between our toes wasn't our idea of fun. But sometimes we kinda liked the poop because it made great ammunition when we were playing war, and the rotten eggs we'd find all around town made dandy stink bombs.

Mrs. Becky Gill, Otis's mom, smiled. "Well, boys, what did you learn in school today?"

I always hated it when adults asked that question. It made me want to ask them what *they'd* learned, but I knew I'd get into trouble if I dared, so I smiled right back at her and told her what I'd learned. "Mr. McGrath told us that the soldiers are having to hide in dirty, muddy, rat-infested trenches and that they're covered in lice and—"

"Yeah," Otis interrupted, "and the trenches are so long that they have to put up signs or the soldiers get lost. They're giving the trenches names like 'Death Valley' and 'Hell Hole.' "

"Otis Leroy Gill! You know better than to use language like that!"

"I can't help it if that's what the trenches are called," Otis said. "I'm not the one who came up with 'Hell Hole.' "

"You may not have come up with that name, but you certainly don't have to repeat it!"

Otis and I looked at each other and grinned. Sometimes our mothers didn't understand that repeating a curse word someone else had said wasn't the same as saying it. There was a big difference. Why didn't they get it? But then again, maybe they did, because repeating a curse word was kind of like being able to curse without the guilt and mothers usually wanted their kids to feel guilty when they said four-letter words.

Hobbling up the front steps and into my house came Aunt Lola. She was the blue-haired, wrinkled-up old lady who lived next door. She wasn't really anybody's aunt, but we called her Aunt Lola because she seemed like a member of the family. She didn't have any relatives close by, and neither did we. All of my aunts and uncles and grandparents lived in Oklahoma, and her two sons lived in California, so Mom and Dad kind of adopted her and made her part of our family on holidays and such. She was always helping out with my baby sister, Daisy, and bringing over all sorts of pies and tarts and goodies.

Daisy took one look at Aunt Lola and held out her arms. "Lo Lo Lo!"

"That's right, Daisy. I'm your Aunt Lo!" She put down her plate of cookies and her walking stick, then picked up Daisy. "How's my sweet-pea precious?"

Daisy yanked on her nose and pulled her hair.

"Ouch! Don't pull hair," Aunt Lola said. "I don't have much, but what I do have, I want to keep!"

Next came Augusta Smith, with her drippy-nosed kids, Melton and Beatrice. For some reason, they always had colds, so we had to keep lots of handkerchiefs around for those two. "Here are some sandwiches," Mrs. Smith said, putting down a plate. "Oh, I love what you've done with the place."

I looked around. Mom had everything shined and polished, with a green cloth on the dining room table and a poinsettia on the windowsill.

"Hello, sisters!" Robyn Burris said, walking in

with little Johnny and a pot of soup. Mom's friends called one another sisters even though they really weren't. It meant they were sister suffragists—ladies who supported the suffrage movement, which proposed that all women have the right to vote. As it was, only eleven states allowed women to vote. Lucky for Mom and her sisters, Oregon had given women the vote in 1912.

As usual, Johnny was picking his nose. "Now, Johnny, sweetie pie. Put your hand down," said Mrs. Burris. Then, to the rest of us, she said in a lower voice, "He's very sensitive about this. We don't want to cause emotional harm. It might hurt his delicate feelings."

Otis and I looked at each other. Then we made a beeline for the front porch to get a breath of fresh air.

"I think little Johnny has more than boogers wrapped around his finger," I told Otis.

Otis laughed, and that's when Miss McKee, the prettiest public librarian anyone ever saw, drove up in her Model T. She jumped out of her auto, hoisting a heaping tray of deviled eggs onto one hip.

"How are my favorite readers today?"

"Fine," I said.

"Fine," Otis replied. "Here, let me help you with that." He ran over to her and took her tray.

Why hadn't I thought of that?

"Say, Corn. I have a new dog book that just arrived," she said. "Would you like me to save it for you?"

"Sure."

Miss McKee knew I liked dogs. She liked them, too. She was always saving me her newest dog books so that I could read them before she put them on the shelf. I thought that was pretty dandy.

Otis walked into the dining room, carrying the tray that I should have been carrying myself. He set it down on the table. "You have anything else to bring in?"

"No, thank you, Otis."

"Come on, kids," I said. "Let's go outside while the ladies play their game."

Beatrice and Melton ran onto the porch. Little Johnny, still picking his nose, followed them. I put Daisy on our porch swing.

"My turn! My turn!" They began shouting and pushing, trying to climb up onto the swing.

Someone had on a smelly diaper. "Who's the stinker?" I asked, looking at Otis.

"Don't look at me!"

We sniffed around until we discovered the culprit.

Oh brother! It was my sister!

Three

"You watch the kids while I go get us some chow," I told Otis after I'd changed Daisy. I handed her to Otis, and she immediately grabbed his nose and yanked his hair.

"Ouch!" he said.

"Oh, I forgot to warn you. Daisy's new trick is pulling hair."

"Now you tell me."

I took the side door into the kitchen. Just as I was about to open the kitchen door to the dining room, I heard Mom say, "Sisters? If we're going to carry this off, we can't tell any man in town. Not our husbands, our brothers, our fathers, not even our sons."

I stopped cold in my tracks. *Sons? What on earth is she talking about?*

"Our next meeting will be tomorrow night, nine o'clock, at the library."

"That's right," Miss McKee said. "Remember the password?"

"Operation Clean Sweep!" the ladies said in unison.

I held my breath and pressed my ear against the door to the dining room.

"Tomorrow night we'll make our nominations," Mom continued.

Nominations? Now I was really confused. *Surely they're not talking about our town election. Those nominations were made a long time ago, and besides, women don't get involved in politics. They must be talking about some kind of women's club. That's it. They're probably talking about the knitting group they're in or their Christmas social to help poor people.*

"I know who I'll be nominating," Mrs. Gill said.

I could hear someone pouring tea. Cups clinked and spoons stirred.

"Flora, you're just the person we need for mayor."

Mayor? I gulped. *Dad is mayor.*

"It would be my honor and pleasure," Mom said.

"Just think, Flora. Your name will go down in history books. People will be reading about you hundreds of years from now—Mayor Flora Sanwick, right here in Umatilla, Oregon. Your name will be up there with all the great suffrage leaders like Elizabeth Cady Stanton and Susan B. Anthony."

I stuck my fingers in both of my ears and wiggled them to make sure I was hearing okay. I was.

"Sister suffragists, I think we stand a very good chance of getting elected," Mom said. "You know there are more women than men in this town. If we spread the word among ourselves, and persuade enough women to vote for us, I think we can give the men of this town a run for their money."

The ladies clinked their teacups and cheered.

"If I'm elected," Mom went on, "the first thing I'm going to do is pay the town's back electric bill and reinstall the streetlights."

I swallowed hard. Ever since Dad had taken office as mayor, he'd refused to pay the electric bill for the streetlights that didn't work. He and the electric company had been going round and round about whose responsibility it was to keep them working. Dad got real mad recently and had his men yank up about half of the lights, which made the streets pretty scary come nighttime.

"Next, I'll make a law against chickens running rampant around town," Mom said. "And then I'll move Elmer's grave!"

Poor ol' Elmer Diffenbottom. His grave was in the middle of Main Street. It used to be in the cemetery, but then Main Street was planned to go right through the part where Elmer had been laid to rest. The men who made the street said they'd move his grave, but they never did. Mom and her sisters were always complaining about it.

Dad had said that the ladies were making a mountain out of a molehill. He didn't seem to mind swerving to miss Elmer's tombstone. He said ol' Elmer gave Main Street lots of character. All the boys agreed with Dad. We thought Elmer's tombstone made a dandy place to sit and think about things. We liked to hang around it and tell ghost stories at night. And rumor had it that it brought good luck, so we always rubbed it right before important events, such as test taking and fish catching and girl kissing.

I didn't know much about that last one, though; girls weren't my specialty. But there was one cute little redhead at school I had my eye on. Her name was Birdine Bain, and every time I saw her, my knees turned weak. She had a whole batch of the prettiest freckles I'd ever seen, sprinkled right across her nose like cinnamon and brown sugar. Sometimes I caught myself looking out the window at school and daydreaming about holding her hand. I just knew it had to be soft.

"Next, I'll fix the boards in the sidewalk," Mom said. "They're a disgrace to this town."

"I agree," Mrs. Smith said. "Have you noticed how bad the sidewalk is in front of Butter Creek Telephone Company? There are three boards missing, and a person who wasn't looking would fall right through!"

Mr. Massie, owner of the telephone company, was known as a penny-pinching ol' geezer. He refused to fix his sidewalk, and he overcharged people for their telephone service.

The side door opened, and in walked Otis, arms crossed, tape measure in hand, with a mad face. "What's takin' so long?" he said.

"Shh," I said. "I'm eavesdropping."

"What for?" He put his ear to the dining room door. "I don't hear nothin'."

"Shh."

"Look, I'm tired of waiting. I've already measured every kid out there *and* the porch swing. I'm hungry. You can eavesdrop all you want, but I'm going in there to get some chow."

Otis pushed open the dining room door, and I tagged behind him.

"Oh, uh, boys! Hello!" Mom said, looking surprised. "How long have you two been standing there?"

"Us? Um, not long." We each grabbed a plate and piled it full of sandwiches, deviled eggs, and cookies. Mom dished up bowls of soup. Then we headed back to the front porch to watch the little nose-pickers and diaper stinkers.

"So?"

"So what?"

"So what were they saying that was so interesting?"

I took a bite of my sandwich and chewed it carefully, thinking about how to reply. "You won't believe it . . . I don't even believe it."

"Try me."

"I can't."

"Since when have you not been able to tell me something?" Otis asked.

He was right. Otis knew everything. He knew about my little brother, who died from smallpox when he was only one month old. He knew about the arrowhead collection under my bed. He even knew about my embarrassing fear of the dark and that I had to have the hall light on to go to sleep and that if he blabbed it to any of the guys in school, he'd be in big trouble.

"What's the deal?"

"Well," I said, taking another bite, "I'm not exactly sure, but it sounds like . . ."

"Like what?"

"Like all the ladies are planning to run for office in our upcoming election and my mom's going to run for mayor!"

Otis lifted his eyebrows. "Very funny, Corncob. You're a real joker. Now tell me the truth."

"I just did, Oatmeal."

"I'm supposed to believe that?" He got out his tape measure and tapped me on the head. "Women don't run for political office, especially for mayor! Come on, Corn. I'm smarter than that!"

"See? I knew you wouldn't believe me."

"A woman can't be mayor! Why, that's—that's a man's job!"

"I know," I said. "They're plumb crazy!"

"They're loony birds!" Otis said, soup dripping down his chin. "How do they expect a man to vote for a woman?"

"Well, that's the thing," I said, drinking my own soup. "According to them, there are more women in this town than men, and if they get most of the women's votes, then they'll win. You think they can really do that?"

Otis shook his head. "Naw! Why would a woman want to vote for another woman when she could vote for a man?"

"Beats me. They were talking about a password and a secret meeting tomorrow night at the library."

"Secret meeting? What's the password?"

"Operation Clean Sweep."

"What the heck is that supposed to mean?"

"I think it means Umatilla is going to get a clean sweep, but not by a broom."

"Then by what?"

"The women."

Four

That night, I lay in bed, tossing and turning. *How can Mom run for mayor? Women don't run for mayor. Especially a woman whose husband is already mayor . . . Women are supposed to be mothers and stay at home. They're supposed to cook and clean and make sure us kids do our homework and don't go around repeating four-letter words without feeling guilty.*

I thought about Mom. *There's no way she can do Dad's job. She's too busy doing her own job here at the house. How does she think she can do her job and Dad's, too? And what about Daisy? Who's gonna watch her? Well, it's not going to be me! There's no way Mom can pull this off. She and her friends are crazier than bed-bugs.*

I thought about Dad. Maybe I should tell him. If it was me running for mayor, I'd sure like to know if my own *wife* was running against me. Wasn't telling Dad the right thing to do? I mean, if Mom knew about Dad, shouldn't Dad know about Mom?

At some point, I must have fallen asleep, because next thing I knew, the sun was shining in my window and the morning smells of bacon and coffee drifted into my room.

I dressed real quick and ran downstairs. Sparky followed right behind, her toenails clicking on each step.

"Mornin', Tiger," Dad said, slathering strawberry jelly onto one of his pancakes.

"Mornin'." I gave Daisy a pat on her curly head. "How's my Daisy Maisy girl?"

Daisy tapped her spoon on the tray of her high chair, stuck out her tongue, and said, "Thhhhhhh-bup."

"You don't say," I said. "Can you say Corn? Co-rn?"

"Coo-Coo!"

"Not Coo-Coo!" I said. "Corn!"

"Do you want two pancakes or three?" Mom asked, standing at the stove.

"Two." I took a bite of bacon, eyeing my parents. They looked pretty normal. I watched Mom as she carefully poured the batter into the skillet and waited until the time was right to flip the pancakes. Her pancakes were always perfect—not too soggy, not overcooked—golden as bubbly sunshine. Mom was meticulous when it came to cooking, and now that I thought of it, she was that way about everything she did. It didn't matter what job she was doing, she always took her time and did it right.

Dad, on the other hand, always seemed to be in a hurry, and he made lots of mistakes. Like the time he built the front porch onto our house. It was a sorry sight, all crooked and slanted, and the roof leaked like a sieve. We were scared to step out on it for the first few weeks, for fear it might cave in, but it never did.

"Corn? Whatcha up to after school?" Dad asked, cutting a triangle of pancake with his fork.

"Well, I'm writing a five-paragraph essay on the Great War, so I'll probably start on that. How about you?"

Dad took another bite of pancake, jelly dripping off the tines of his fork. "Let's see, now . . . I've got another meeting with the council, and an election debate with Lanier. Then I've got to pick up my posters and start posting them all around town. Want to help out?"

I glanced at Mom, who had finally taken her place at the table. Her face didn't show any signs of sneakiness. "Um, maybe."

"Maybe?" Dad looked surprised. "You don't want to help your old man?"

"Sure I do. I was just thinking, though, I'll probably have to go to the library to do my work."

"Oh, I see," Dad said. "Okay, then."

"Dad?" I put down my fork, thinking. "Um, do you like being mayor? I mean, do you really like it?" I looked at Mom to see if she would squirm in her chair, but she didn't.

Dad glanced at Mom, then at me. "Well, I don't *love* it, if that's what you mean. But I like it. Being mayor is hard work. It may look easy, but there's a lot that goes into it, which most folks don't realize."

That was when Mom got interested. "Like what, Frank?"

Dad rubbed his chin. "Well, let's see. Take Sticky Fingers Fred, for instance. Not only am I trying to run a town, plan an election, organize a parade, and campaign, but now I have to see that a dingdong pickpocket doesn't crash our parade."

Mom gave Daisy a bite of pancake. "Why don't you post a man at both entrances to town? That way you can keep a lookout for anyone unusual."

"That's what I'm doing," Dad said. "I've got two men lined up to be there at eight in the morning on the day of the parade."

Mom's eyes looked thoughtful. "Frank? I think you should post them there the day *before* the parade. If this fellow's a professional, like the newspapers claim he is, he'd probably arrive a day early to survey our town and learn his way around."

"I don't have the manpower to do it. The day before the election, I've got everyone busy."

Mom sighed. "Just the same, Frank, I'd find a way."

•

As usual, Otis and I walked to school, meeting up with each other at Elmer's tombstone. The November wind was so cold my nose dripped, my breath fogged the air, and I wished I had worn my mittens.

"Did you know our math book is nine inches by eleven inches?"

"Would you stop!"

"Stop what?"

"Going around measuring everything."

Otis wound up his tape measure. "You're just jealous."

"Jealous? Of what? That tape measure?"

"My *spring-loaded, nickel-plated* tape measure," Otis corrected.

I laughed. Sometimes Otis took that tape measure of his too seriously.

"So did you tell your dad?" Otis asked.

"No."

"No? Why not?"

I shrugged. "Don't know."

"What do you mean, you don't know?" Otis grabbed my hand and made it rub Elmer's tombstone. "There. Now you've got good luck. Tell your dad."

"If I tell, I'll feel like a traitor. And if I don't tell, I'll feel like a traitor."

Otis let out a foggy breath. "What's your gut telling you to do?" He kicked a tumbleweed as we walked along.

"That's just it. I don't know. I'm torn. Part of me wants to tell, but part of me doesn't. Believe me, either way I lose." I gave his tumbleweed a good hard kick.

We walked past the Butter Creek Telephone Company, being careful to step over the missing boards in the sidewalk, the Gem Saloon, and the Tum-A-Lum Lumber Yard, and came to the ferry. Sam Burris, the ferry operator, was loading up a Model T to take to the other side of the Columbia River.

Little Johnny, his son, was sitting on the side of the ferry, his legs dangling. "Hey, Sam!" I called.

"Hey, Corn!"

"Hey, Sam!" Otis called. "What's the weather today?"

"Thirty-two degrees! It's snowing in Pendleton and headed this way!"

We waved and watched him load the Model T up the ramp and onto the ferry, then begin his journey to the Washington side of the river. His ferry was propelled by a horse and a mule, Tip and Nip, who were brothers—actually half brothers, because Nip's daddy was a donkey. Tip had a white streak on his face and his nose was soft as velvet. Nip had long shaggy ears, which showed the donkey in him.

All day long, Tip and Nip walked around and around in a sixteen-foot circle at the front of the ferry with a bar attached to their backs. The bar set in motion a series of paddles under the ferry, which made the ferry go back and forth between Oregon and Washington. Sometimes, though, Nip decided to stop midriver and refused to walk until Sam gave him what he wanted—an oatmeal cookie with raisins, and it had to have raisins. How that mule knew the difference between a plain oatmeal cookie and one with raisins was beyond me.

The ferry was quite a sight to see, which is why I knew that when I grew up I wanted to operate one, just like Sam.

"You boys have a good day!" Sam hollered.

"You too!" we yelled back. "Bye, Johnny!" Then we ran the rest of the way to school.

Five

Mr. McGrath discussed our five-paragraph essays, which were due next Monday. He said we had to write an introduction with three facts about the war, then three paragraphs that supported these facts, and a conclusion that wrapped it all together.

"I want a bibliography, too," he said, giving us a stern look. "No listing sources you didn't use. I'll be checking sources."

The class moaned and groaned, but not me. I didn't mind writing an essay. I kinda liked writing. It was fun to see what I could come up with.

Birdine, the cute little redhead with freckles, glanced my way. She smiled. If she wasn't so gosh-darn pretty, I'd take her on as a friend, but I didn't quite know how to treat a girl, especially one who made my knees weak. I smiled back, then looked down at my desk.

Our next subject was history. My favorite. Lately we'd been discussing the gold rush in Oregon during the 1850s and 1860s and how shiploads of Chinese men had moved into Umatilla and nearby Pendleton either to work on the railroads or to pan for gold.

"Does anyone here know about the sundown law?" Mr. McGrath asked, sitting on the edge of his desk. He had a sly smile, as if he was about to surprise us.

"This law started during the gold rush. You see, white men didn't like the Chinese, who moved here as soon as gold was discovered. The white men felt threatened by the large numbers of Chinese and unfortunately treated them like dogs. They even went so far as to create the sundown law, which stated that if any Chinese man—or any person of color—was out after sundown, a white man had the right to shoot him."

Everyone gasped. What a crummy law! How could that be legal?

"Well, the Chinese men were stuck here. Many of them had spent their last penny getting to Oregon. They couldn't just turn around and go home because the white men didn't like them. So they decided to make the best of their situation and dug underground tunnels in both Umatilla and Pendleton, creating their own world. These tunnels led to Chinese laundries, saloons, and gambling houses. Pendleton's tunnels also had an underground jail, so that if anyone had too much to drink and started to go up into the streets, the Chinese authorities would lock him in and let him sleep it off. The Chinese had opium dens, too. These were small rooms where the men would smoke opium, a drug that causes hallucinations."

Birdine raised her hand and said, "My daddy found one of their smoking pipes in an underground tunnel when he was a boy. He still has it."

Then all the kids started raising their hands, telling of Chinese items they had found, coins and cups and game pieces. I told about coins I had dug up over by Sam's ferry.

"Next week I'd like you to bring in your Chinese artifacts, and be prepared to discuss what you know about them," Mr. McGrath said.

I smiled. Talking about my coin collection would be easy.

•

"What are you going to write about for your essay on the Great War?" Birdine asked at lunch. She sat down at the desk next to mine. Opening her lunch pail, she pulled out a piece of fried chicken, an apple, and a biscuit oozing butter and grape jelly.

I looked down at my desk. "Me? Um, I'm writing about, um, animals and how they're using them on the front lines. How about you?"

She took a bite of her chicken. "I haven't decided yet. But I'm thinking of writing about the pigeons or maybe the—"

"I'm writing about the pigeons," I said, looking up real fast. "The pigeons and the dogs."

Our eyes met. She had pretty eyes, kinda brown and green mixed together.

"Well, then," she said, "maybe I'll write about the horses."

"Horses are good."

"They have to wear gas masks just like the men, you know."

I opened my lunch pail and took out five crackers, a chunk of cheese, some sausage, a carrot, and a slice of blueberry pie.

"Gee, that looks good. Wanna trade?"

Our eyes met again, and I felt kinda loopy. "Trade? Um, okay. What do you want to trade?"

"My biscuit for your blueberry pie."

Now, any boy in his right mind would have known

that *that* was a bad trade. That was as bad as it got. Even worse than the time Otis traded his bologna sandwich for a half-eaten, dropped-in-the-dirt apple. But being that her eyes were so pretty and her freckles so cute, I handed her my pie.

"Mmm. This is good," she said. "So are you going to the library after school to start your research?"

I looked around the room, wondering where Otis was. *Why is he letting me flounder and trade my good blueberry pie for some dumb ol' biscuit? Where is he when I need him?*

Otis smiled and waved from his spot at the back of the room. He had sat down by some of the guys, and they were all poking fun at me—blowing kisses, batting their eyes, and making a kissing sound. I could tell I was on my own this time.

"Um, uh, I'm sorry. What did you ask?"

"I said, are you going to the library after school?"

Her freckles made me think of cinnamon toast. I swallowed hard and looked back down at my lunch. "Um, I guess so."

"Good," she said, smiling. "Then I'll see you there."

That was what I was afraid of. Me and Birdine. At the library. Together. Maybe even sitting at the same table.

Six

"Corn and Birdine sitting in a tree.
K-i-s-s-i-n-g!
First comes love, then comes marriage,
Then comes Birdine with a—"

"Funny," I said. "Very funny."

"So when's the wedding?"

"There's not going to be any wedding," I told Otis after school.

"Look, Corn. I happen to know that you traded your blueberry pie for her biscuit. Now, if that ain't love, I don't know what is!"

"I happen to like biscuits."

"Since when? You never traded blueberry pie for one of *my* biscuits." Otis got out his tape measure and pointed it at my heart. "You're in love, aren't ya?"

"Would you stop?" I looked him in the eye. "She wanted to trade, so I traded. Over and done with. And you weren't there to help me! All right?"

"All right." But he was still smirking, and I didn't like it.

"Come on, let's go to the library to do our research," I said. We walked out the door of the schoolhouse.

“I still can’t decide what to write about.”

Since writing came easy to me, I tossed out some ideas. “Write about the trenches. Or the submarine warfare. I know, how about the airplanes? This is the first war with air combat, you know.”

We walked along. “Hey, look!” I said, picking up an arrowhead.

Otis and I inspected it. It was in good shape, all notched along the edges and made of shale. He got out his measuring tape again. “Two and three-fourths inches. That’s a good size.”

Otis and I were always on the lookout for arrowheads and stuff. Sometimes, on Saturday mornings, we’d meet real early on the bank of the Columbia River with our moms’ flour sifters, sifting for what we could find in the sand—Chinese coins, arrowheads, shells, Indian sinkers.

I’d already collected about a dozen sinkers. These were rocks that the Indians used to sink their fishing lines down into the water. They were round and flat, like the kind we used for skipping, only the Indians would carve a notch on the top and bottom for their lines to wrap into.

“So what do you think our mothers are going to do at this secret meeting tonight?” Otis asked.

"I guess they're going to make their nominations," I said. "You think your mom will get nominated?"

"My mom? That's a laugh!"

"Don't laugh," I said. "They're serious. You know mine's running for mayor!"

Otis eyed me. "Whose side are you on?"

"Nobody's."

"Well, I'm on the men's side. I think you should be, too."

"Easy for you to say. Your dad isn't mayor, and your mom isn't *running* for mayor."

"So. I'd still be on the men's side, no matter what."

"All right, all right, I'm on the men's side. Happy now?"

Otis nudged me. "Are you gonna tell your dad?"

"I haven't decided. And don't you tell him, either."

"Okay."

"Promise?"

"Promise."

Leaves crunched under our shoes as we passed the Tum-A-Lum, where lumber and wagon wheels were stacked out front. Seeing Mahoney's Drug Store, we looked at each other with the same idea.

"Got a nickel?"

"Yeah. Do you?"

Otis searched his pocket. "Aw shucks! All I've got is my tape measure and this note."

"Note? Who wrote you a note?" I leaned over his shoulder.

"Nobody," Otis said, stuffing it back into his pocket.

"Nobody? Well, Nobody sure has pretty cursive. Let's see, who could that be?"

"None of your business!"

I smiled. Otis could dish it out, but he sure couldn't take it. "Come on, let's go get a chocolate soda with two straws."

We walked into Mahoney's and sat on the shiny red stools that spun around in circles.

"Howdy, boys! What'll it be?" Mrs. Goode asked, wiping off the counter.

"The usual," I said, "but this time only one, with two straws."

"And two cherries, please," Otis added.

We watched Mrs. Goode squirt three streams of chocolate syrup, then drop a dollop of whipped cream, a sprinkle of cocoa, and some soda water into a metal shaker and mix it all together. Then she poured it into a tall glass and topped it off with more whipped cream, a bit of nutmeg, two cherries, and just enough cherry juice to drip down into the dark chocolaty syrup.

"You think we should go to that meeting tonight?" Otis asked.

"Us? No boys allowed, remember?" We took turns taking sips, only I noticed that Otis's sips were longer than mine, so I started taking longer sips to try to catch up.

Otis stopped sipping. He opened his mouth and his eyes got real big, as though he'd just had a great idea. "But what if we went to their meeting and nobody knew?"

"How?"

He rubbed his chin. "We could sneak in."

"Yeah, and if our moms caught us, we'd be dead meat."

"Well, we could *peek* in."

"Peek in? That's a two-story building."

"I'll bring a ladder."

"Hey," I said. "That's a good idea. While we're at the library today, why don't we open a window, just a teeny-tiny bit? That way, if their meeting is on the second floor, we could lean the ladder up against the building and listen through the window."

"Good thinking," Otis said, spinning his stool in a full circle.

I spun mine, too.

"Let's meet at nine o'clock. Elmer's tombstone."

We shook on it, then we spun on it.

Otis took one last long sip, finishing up our soda.

"Gee, Otis. You could have left some for me, you know."

"I did." He tilted the glass. "See? There's one drop left."

"Thanks a lot," I said, giving him a mean look. "Next time, our chocolate soda is on *your* nickel."

Seven

On July 28, 1914, the Great War began in Europe and continues to claim the lives of more and more soldiers. Since no one wants to carry messages to the soldiers fighting on the front lines for fear of getting shot at, many animals are being used for this purpose, including war dogs, carrier pigeons, and postal pigeons.

There. I reread what I had written. Not too shabby. That took care of my introduction. Now for my three supporting paragraphs. I chewed on my pencil, looked through more newspapers, and thought some more.

The Germans are using specially trained dogs called war dogs, *which carry messages in containers on their collars. These dogs must wear gas masks because of a new weapon—poison gas—a thick, greenish-yellow gas that rolls over the ground like a mist, killing every soldier and every animal in its path without a gas mask.*

Carrier pigeons are also being used to deliver messages to soldiers on the front lines. But because of all the noise—guns, tanks, machine guns—the pigeons often get confused and fly in wrong directions. The poison gas causes a problem for them, too. I guess they don't make gas masks tiny enough for them.

I tapped my pencil. I gave it a good chewing until nearly all the yellow paint had crumbled off. I picked the pieces out of my teeth and flicked them onto the floor. *Let's see now. Where am I? Pigeons. Oh yeah.*

Postal pigeons with secret messages and battle strategy attached to their legs are being dropped by tiny parachutes into occupied areas. Soldiers are deciphering these messages, writing their replies, and sending the pigeons back to their leaders, informing them of how the battles are going and how their soldiers are holding up.

Many animals are being used in the effort to win the Great War. Hundreds of war dogs, carrier pigeons, and postal pigeons are losing their lives daily to get messages to the soldiers on the front lines. But it doesn't seem fair. Why kill innocent animals? They're not the ones who started this Great War. And I don't think it should be called the Great War. What's so "great" about killing people and animals?

"How's your essay coming?"

I looked up. There stood Birdine, pretty as a postcard, her freckles looking every bit like cinnamon and brown sugar. "Um, it's coming along really good. It's about finished. Now I, um, need to check it over."

"Gee, you're lucky. I wish I was finished."

I smiled, but only because I couldn't think of what to say.

"Isn't this war awful?" Birdine asked. "I wish there was no such thing."

"Me too."

Otis sat down next to me, scrunching up his nose and looking disgusted. "See this?" He showed us pictures of soldiers, standing knee-deep in water-filled trenches. In one photo, three soldiers in a trench were standing on top of dead bodies. I had to look away.

About that time, Miss McKee came over to our table. "Here are my favorite readers," she said. "What are you three up to today?"

"We're writing essays on the Great War," I said.

Miss McKee frowned. "My little brother, Luke, enlisted in the army. I'm worried he'll have to go off and fight soon."

Otis showed her the pictures. "It says right here that the Germans and the Allies have each already lost nearly a million men."

I kicked Otis under the table.

"Ouch! What'd you go and do that for?"

I shot him a dirty look. Miss McKee was already worried; she didn't need Otis making things worse. Sometimes Otis didn't use his head.

Miss McKee handed me a book called *Dogs: Man's Best Friend*. "I think you'll like this one. There's a dog in there that kinda looks like your dog."

"Gee, thanks." I thumbed through the book.

"I just love dogs," Birdine said. "I read about them all the time."

"You do?" I looked into her eyes. "What's your favorite book?"

"*The Dogs from Bakersfield*."

"That's *my* favorite book. Have you read the new one called *The Bakersfield Dogs Return*? It's even better than the first one."

"Gee, do you have it?" she asked. "I'm on the waiting list to get it from the library, but it's taking too long."

Miss McKee smiled real big and pretty as she handed Birdine a book.

"*The Bakersfield Dogs Return*! Thanks, Miss McKee."

"I just got it in this morning. I knew you'd be pleased. Well, good luck on your essays," Miss McKee said. "If you need any help, let me know."

There was something I wanted to know, but it didn't have anything to do with our essays. It had to do with my mother's running for office. "Miss McKee?"

"Yes, Cornelius?"

"Well, um, I was wondering . . . since you're a girl and all, what do you think about women and politics?"

Her eyebrows rose. "Why, Cornelius, I didn't know you had an interest in politics."

"Oh yeah, I'm real interested." And it wasn't a lie, either.

"Well, things are changing. Did you know that Oregon women who tried to vote before it became legal were thrown in jail? Now those women are voting legally. What used to be a man's world is opening up to women. Eleven states have given women the right to vote so far."

I nodded. "My mom says that soon all states will give women the vote."

"That's right, but only if we keep pushing for it. Men don't want to give up their power. I guess they think women shouldn't concern themselves with such weighty matters. But I say women can make decisions just as well as or better than men, and we have every right to vote." She hesitated, then said, "We even have a right to run for office."

"Really?" I asked. Now we were getting somewhere. "You think a woman can do just as well in office as a man?"

"Most certainly," she said. "Why wouldn't she?"

"Be-because she's a woman?" I asked, fidgeting with my pencil.

"And what does that mean?"

Birdine jumped in, smiling. "Yeah. What's that supposed to mean?"

Now I was really fidgeting, all the way down to my toes. "Well, um . . ." I looked at Otis. He looked at me.

"Let me put it this way," Miss McKee said. "Let's say you have a town where no people live, only dogs and cats. And let's say these dogs and cats want to make public decisions about where they live and how to better their future. Is it right to let only the cats make the decisions and not the dogs?"

I shook my head. "Because then the cats might only make decisions that benefit them and not the dogs."

"Exactly," Miss McKee said. "And shouldn't the dogs have their say in things, too?"

I nodded.

"There you have it. That's why women should be able to vote, and that's why we should be able to run for public office. It's the democratic way."

I looked at Otis and Birdine. If they didn't know what the word *democratic* meant, they sure didn't show it. I wasn't going to be the only one not knowing, so I decided to look it up in the dictionary when I got home.

Eight

Democratic—adj. 1. Of or for all the people.
2. Considering and treating others as one's equals.
3. Belonging to a democracy.

I smacked the dictionary shut. "See, Dirl? You don't want those cats making all the decisions, do you?"

Sparky put her head in my lap. Her stump of a tail wagged.

"But if the democratic way is right, how come the women are sneaking around behind the men's backs? Shouldn't they be honest and say, *Here we are! We're running for office, just like the men*?"

Sparky held out her paw.

"Good, Dirl! Shake?"

She shook.

"Speak. Speak."

Sparky let out a little woof.

"That's my Dirl."

Good smells from the kitchen made their way up into my bedroom, reminding me that it was suppertime.

"Let's eat!" Mom called.

I bounded down the steps, but Sparky knew what "Let's eat!" meant, too, and she took off faster than a train and was sitting at her usual spot under my chair when I got there. "Dirl? How did you do that?"

Sparky just looked at me as if I was a slowpoke.

"Yah-goo-bah," Daisy said, holding out her tiny fist. She was looking at a plate of turnip greens. If she knew what they were, she probably wouldn't act so excited.

I put a couple of the slimy green pieces onto her tray, and she smiled as if I'd just given her something special. I held back my laugh when she picked up one piece and put it into her mouth. Her eyebrows scrunched, her face looked surprised, and she instantly spit it out, all down her front.

I laughed. "Daisy Maisy girl doesn't like turnip greens?"

Her eyes watered, and drool dripped off her chin.

"Okay, then how about this?" I handed her a little chunk of corn bread and a sliver of ham. She looked at me as if she didn't trust me. "It's okay, Daisy. I promise, you'll like this."

The food went right to her mouth, and she tapped her tray with her spoon for more.

I watched both of my parents as they took their

places at the table—Mom in her long black skirt with a white ruffled blouse, looking thin, and pretty in a tired sort of way; Dad in his starched shirt, woolen pants, and suspenders, looking hefty and a lot older than Mom, though he was really three years younger.

"Tiger," Dad said, handing me the front page of the newspaper, "looks like ol' Sticky Fingers Fred hit another town last night."

"Oh no!"

"Not again!" Mom said. "Read it out loud." She cut up more pieces of ham for Daisy and put them on her tray.

I laid the paper on the table and began to read:

"STICKY STICKS CECIL

"November 30, 1916—Sticky Fingers Fred, the most notorious pickpocket in the West, struck the town of Cecil last night during a chili contest, which helped to raise over forty-eight dollars for the town's new Christmas decorations.

"With fourteen steaming pots full of delicious chili and five sheets of corn bread, guests purchased a twenty-five-cent ticket for all they could eat, but their chili supper ended up costing much more than many expected."

Daisy banged her tray with her spoon, sending a piece of ham flying through the air, right onto my forehead. "Aw, Daisy. What'd you do that for?"

Mom and Dad laughed. I slipped the ham to Sparky, who didn't seem to mind one bit that it had Daisy drool all over it. I wiped my forehead with my napkin and finished reading, keeping one eye on Daisy, the ham launcher.

> *"Without the townspeople knowing, this trickster took money, watches, and jewelry totalling over three hundred dollars' worth of stolen valuables, even going so far as to steal the diamond bobs off a woman's ears.*
>
> *" 'My husband, Larry, gave them to me on our first anniversary,' stated an angry Mrs. Carol Large, with tears in her eyes. 'I've had those earbobs for over forty-four years, and I want that lily-livered lawbreaker behind bars!'*
>
> *"Cecil sheriff Scott Carter said, 'We didn't even see the guy. We were on the lookout for him, too. But one of our staff did notice a rather tall woman with a blue hat and a large handbag, wobbling on high-heeled shoes.'*
>
> *"Wrapping up the month of November, this makes the eleventh town hit in the last eight*

months. It appears this lowlife is headed east through Oregon. All towns are to be on the alert. A $500.00 reward is offered for information leading to his capture. An additional $100.00 reward is now offered by Mr. and Mrs. Larry Large of Cecil."

I put down the newspaper. "Can you believe this guy?"

Dad shook his head. "He's pretty desperate, isn't he?"

"I should say," Mom said, scrunching her lips.

"So how's your essay coming along?" Dad asked.

"Fine. It's about finished." I took a bite of my turnip greens. They were awful and slimy and slid down my throat like slugs. "Do I *have* to eat these?"

"If you want dessert."

"What's for dessert?"

"Lemon tarts with cream."

Mmm. I pinched my nose and took another bite, then washed it down real quick with milk.

"What did you decide to write about?" Mom asked.

"Pigeons and dogs and how they're using them on the front lines." I sneaked Sparky a handful of turnip greens, but she wasn't dumb. She took one sniff and moved under Daisy's high chair. "You know, I just don't get it. Why do we have to fight? Why can't countries solve their problems without going around killing innocent people and animals?"

Mom and Dad looked at each other, then at me.

Mom's lips tightened and her nose got that pointy look it always got when she was real serious about something. "I can't understand it, either, Corn. But I can tell you this: if countries were run by women, there would be no war."

"Now, Flora honey, you don't know that."

"Don't Flora honey me, Frank. If women were in government, they'd rule with their hearts, not their muscles."

"And a lot of good that would do us—a bunch of crying women, sitting around gossiping and complaining."

"Gossiping and complaining?" Mom pointed her fork at Dad. "I'm sure men gossip and complain even more than women."

Oh brother! Here they go again.

"And how would you know that?" Dad asked, smiling.

"Easy," Mom said, smiling right back. "I live with you." She stood and started clearing the dishes. "Oh, that reminds me, Frank. Aunt Lola is sick, and I need to go check on her tonight."

"Sick?" Dad asked. "That's a shame. What's she got?"

"Flu, I suspect."

I'd never caught Mom in an outright lie before, at least not that I knew of, and now that I had, I didn't feel very good.

"I'll be over there for quite a while," Mom said, looking down. "So don't wait up for me."

"And who's going to watch our little hair-puller?"

"Why, you are, Frank." She smiled, then bent down and kissed his bald spot. "You're not going to *complain*, are you?"

"Me? Complain? Never."

•

At ten minutes until nine o'clock, when I was upstairs checking my essay, I heard the front door open and then click shut. I ran to my window and watched as Mom walked down the dark street, past Aunt Lola's house—which had a few lights left on, probably to fool Dad—and around the corner and out of sight.

My heart pounded—it was time for me to leave, too. Otis had said that he'd meet me at Elmer's tombstone at exactly nine, but I hadn't thought of an excuse to tell Dad. I ran through my list of usual excuses for getting out at night. *I forgot my math book*? *I need to borrow a paper from Otis*? *Sparky needs to go for a walk*? That one would work. I bolted downstairs.

"Dad? Sparky wants to go for a walk. Is that okay with you?"

Sparky, hearing the magic word *walk*, ran around in circles, then to the door.

Dad looked over his newspaper. Daisy was crawling around by his feet. She had pulled off one of his socks and was sucking on it. "I suppose. Don't be gone too long."

"I won't."

I put Sparky's leash on her, and out we went into the cold night air.

Nine

Sparky and I walked along the dark street, being sure to keep out of the light from the few streetlights that were working. Hanky Panky, Aunt Lola's yellow tomcat, came walking down the sidewalk and sniffed at my pant legs.

"Hey, Hanky! How's Hanky Panky doin'?"

He rubbed against my legs and came nose to nose with Sparky.

"Dirl? Be nice."

The hair on her neck stood up.

"Dirl? Come on. Let's go." I yanked on her leash, almost choking her to pull her away. Last time she and Hanky Panky came nose to nose, she took off after that cat as if she'd been shot out of a cannon, and I had no choice but to hang on for dear life. That dog of mine took me through three backyards, a flower bed, and a clothesline before Hanky Panky climbed a fence and got away.

We walked along, Sparky stopping in almost every yard to smell around and relieve herself. How one dog could go to the bathroom that much was beyond me. She must stock up all day, just waiting for her nightly walk.

When we got to our destination, Otis was sitting on Elmer's tombstone, tape measure in hand. "Did you know it's nineteen and six-eighths inches from my heel to my knee?" he asked.

There he goes again. Mr. Tape Measure.

"Want me to measure Sparky's leash?"

"Um, no thanks."

He ignored me and measured it, anyway. "Six feet five inches."

"Will you wind that thing up?" I asked. "You're driving me crazy with it."

Giving me a mean look, he put it in his coat pocket. "Are you ready? I've got the ladder hidden in that bush over there."

We both gave Elmer's tombstone a good hard rub, then each picked up an end of the ladder and walked down the street, slinking in the shadows and looking over our shoulders to make sure no one was watching. Sparky pulled us along, as though she knew where we were headed. When we got to the Umatilla Public Library, we were careful to take the street behind it and sneak up through the alley.

"Which window did you open?" Otis whispered as we looked at the rectangles of light streaming from the windows on the second floor.

Gee, looking up from down here in the grass, I wasn't too sure. At first I thought it was the one on the far left, but then I thought it might be the second from the left.

"Come on. Which is it? We don't have all night, you know."

"Um, I think it's the second from the left."

"You *think*? You mean you don't know for sure?"

"Well, they look alike from down here. Let's try that one."

We quietly leaned the ladder up against the wall. Otis steadied the legs. "There. Now go on up and see if this is the right window."

"Me? You go up!"

"You're the one who doesn't know which window you opened," Otis whispered. "Go ahead."

I gave Otis Sparky's leash and slowly climbed the ladder. When I got to the twelfth rung, I looked down at Otis and Sparky and felt a little bit dizzy.

"Don't look down!" Otis said. "Just keep going."

I held on with both hands, getting shakier and shakier. I reached the window. It wasn't open. I started back down.

"Wrong window," I whispered. We pulled the ladder from the wall carefully, so it didn't make a sound, and slowly moved it under the next window. But there was a hole in the ground under that window, and the ladder wouldn't stand straight.

"Don't worry," Otis said. "I'll hold it and make sure you don't fall."

"You?" I asked. "Why don't I get to hold it and you climb up this time?"

"Because it's my ladder."

"So?"

"So climb on up there."

"But what if I fall?" I didn't want to sound like a baby, but seeing the size of that hole and feeling how wobbly the ladder was made me nervous.

Otis huffed, kicking some dirt and leaves into the hole. "There. Is that better?"

I kicked some more dirt into the hole and stomped it down with my boot, then set one leg of the ladder over it. Gingerly, I climbed up, taking each step real slow. When I got to the window, it was open about an inch and I had a perfect view.

"Do you see anything?"

"Yeah!" I said softly.

"What do you see?"

"A bunch of women flying around on brooms!"

Otis cracked up. "You do not! Now tell me!"

I looked inside. All the women were standing around, chitchatting and drinking punch. "They're having a big brawl and, oh my, you should see them fight! Aunt Lola just punched your mom in the nose!"

"Corncob? Quit joking or I'm going to let go of this ladder!" He gave the ladder a jolt, making me hold on tightly.

"All right. All right. They're taking their seats . . . My mom is standing at the podium, holding a broom in the air . . . She's saying, 'Sister suffragists! This town needs a clean sweep!' "

"How many's in there?" Otis whispered.

I tried to count. "Twenty. Maybe thirty."

Sparky didn't like my being up on the ladder without her. She tried to climb the first few rungs, then fell down with a yelp.

"Shh, Dirl! Stay down."

"What else?" Otis asked.

"Now they're taking nominations, and your mom just nominated my mom for mayor . . . Oh no! You're not going to like this."

"What? What?"

"Your mom!"

"What about her?"

"She just got nominated for treasurer."

"Oh brother! How can she do this to me?"

The ladder wobbled. "Hey! Watch what you're doin' down there!"

"It's Sparky!" Otis said. "She keeps trying to climb the ladder! Make her stop!"

Right about that time, Sparky began whining. She whined and whined, and Otis let go of the ladder.

"Hey! Hold on to the—"

But it was too late. The ladder fell, and I came tumbling down, landing in a pile of leaves.

"Corn? Are you okay?"

I opened my eyes. Sparky was licking my face. "Yeah."

Otis helped me to my feet, but I didn't feel so good. My shoulder ached. My head was spinning.

"You want me to go up now?" Otis asked.

"I'm not going back up there."

We tried to lean the ladder against the building as quietly as we could, but it made a thud.

"Shh!" we said to each other. Then I threatened Sparky with a mean look. "That goes for you, too, Miss Big Mouth!"

Sparky held out her paw.

"I'm not shaking hands with you, Dirl. You just made me fall off this ladder."

I steadied the ladder as Otis climbed it. He stood there for a long time, not saying anything.

"Well? What's going on?"

"You won't believe it!"

"What?"

"They really *are* flying!"

"Oh, come on!"

"All right. They're marching around the room with brooms, sweeping from right to left, saying, 'Clean sweep! Clean sweep! This town needs a clean sweep!' I guess they're going to march in the election day parade with their brooms . . . Oh no!"

"What?"

"Birdine just walked by, and she looked up at the window."

"Birdine? What's she doing in there?"

"Don't know, but she has paint on her hands and face. Must be painting a sign or something. Now she's looking again."

"Are you sure?"

"Sure I'm sure." He ducked down. Then he peeked back in. "Oh no!"

"Oh no what?"

"She's talking to her mother and pointing at the window. Let's get out of here!" He scrambled down, jumping from the halfway point, and we made a beeline for some nearby bushes, forgetting something very important—the ladder.

We ran back, grabbed the ladder, and took off into the bushes just as Birdine came running around the corner. She walked under the window where our ladder had stood. She crossed her arms. "I know you're out here!" she shouted, looking around. "And you better not repeat anything you heard!" Then she went back inside.

"Gee, that was close."

"I'll say. You think she knew it was us?"

"Maybe."

"So what are we going to do if she says something about it?" Otis asked.

"The only thing decent respectable boys like us *can* do."

"What's that?"

"Lie like a dog and deny it."

Ten

That night I lay in bed with the hall light on and Sparky at my feet. My shoulder ached; my head still throbbed. I worried about Birdine recognizing us. *What if she tells her mother? What if she figures out that if Otis was at the top of the ladder, then I was probably at the bottom? She really can't prove anything. Can she? I mean, it was dark.*

Next morning, at breakfast, Mom rubbed liniment on my aching shoulder. "How did you hurt your shoulder?"

My heart skipped a beat. "Um, well . . . it happened last night." Which was no lie.

Dad poured milk into our glasses. "Did it happen on your walk with Sparky?"

"Yeah."

"You know how Sparky is," Dad said to Mom. "She just jerks Corn all around town like a puppet on a string. I'll bet that's how it happened."

"Yeah, she's the reason for this, all right." That wasn't a lie, either. If she hadn't started whining, Otis wouldn't have let go of the ladder and I wouldn't have fallen.

We ate our breakfast. Cornflakes and toast with cinnamon and sugar sprinkled on top. My thoughts turned to Birdine.

"Would you believe what that ol' mud-slinging Lanier had the gall to do?" Dad asked, slurping his coffee.

"What?" Mom asked.

Daisy pounded her tray with her spoon.

"Well, yesterday I was hanging posters around town. They turned out real good, by the way, and had my photo on them. Anyway, that scalawag put up his posters right on top of mine. Can you believe that?"

Mom sighed.

I just sat there, thinking more and more about

Birdine's cinnamon-sprinkled face. *But what if she's on to me and accuses me of peeking in on their secret meeting? I wish I didn't have to see her at school today.*

"Just pull his posters down," Mom said. "He shouldn't have done that."

"I know. And that's just what I did. I yanked down all his posters. But he went around putting them back up, right over mine again. Then we got into an argument on the street corner. He said I was a dirty, rotten, tax-raising, yellow-bellied Democrat!"

"He didn't."

"He did!"

"So what did you say?"

"I called him a tightfisted, beady-eyed, tax-hating Republican and said that if he ran this town we wouldn't have a penny in our budget!"

"You didn't," Mom said, covering her smile.

"I sure did. You know he's only running against me because of what happened in high school, don't you?"

That's when I jumped in. "We know, we know." Mom and I had heard that story a million times, and if I had to hear it again, I'd croak. As the story went, Dad was captain of the football team. Apparently, Kim

Lanier wanted that position. Since he didn't get it, he went for Dad's girlfriend, who was Mom. He didn't get her, either. Ever since then, those two had been at each other's throats. You'd think that two grown men wouldn't act so childish, but sometimes parents acted more like children than children did.

We finished our breakfast and Dad dropped me off at school in our Model T. I opened the door, feeling a gust of wind hit my face. I started to get out, but didn't.

"Um, Dad?"

"Yes, son?"

"I was just wondering: what will you do if more people vote for Lanier than for you?"

Dad scowled. "Well, let's hope that doesn't happen. I have to admit, though, I've been a little worried, with him going around covering up my posters and spreading lies about me. Did you know he's been telling folks that if I get reelected, the first thing I plan to do is raise taxes? Can you believe that dirty, rotten lie?"

I shook my head.

"The gall of that guy," Dad continued. "He even told one old lady that I plan to make old folks pay *double* taxes!"

"Da-ad. What I'm asking is, would it bother you not to be mayor, I mean if someone *else* beats you?"

"If that someone else is that scoundrel Lanier, it would."

"But, um, what if it wasn't him? What if it was, oh, someone else?"

Dad looked at me kind of funny-like. "What are you trying to say, Corn?"

I swallowed the lump in my throat. "Well, I'm just wondering, if you were up against someone *besides* him—you know, someone *else*—would it bother you if that someone else won?"

"Hmmm." Dad scratched his bald spot, thinking. "Probably not, if that other person was capable of being a good mayor, but believe me, that Lanier can't think about anyone but himself! He's the stingiest, the rottenest, the—"

"Do you think that maybe, if you didn't win, you'd have more time to take me fishing like you used to? And maybe, if you wanted to, we could whistle duets in church again, like we used to?"

Dad looked at me and winced. "I guess it's been a while. When was the last time we went fishing? A couple of weeks ago?"

"Three months, one week, and four days," I said, looking down at my shoes.

That's when Dad hugged me. Right there, in front of the school, with everybody watching. "I'm sorry, son. I didn't realize how caught up I've been in my job lately. I promise, I'll try to do better."

"That's okay, Dad." But it wasn't. I really wanted him to spend time with me, the way he used to before he became mayor.

"Say," Dad said, "do you think you could do me a favor after school today?"

"Sure."

He handed me one of his posters. "Could you put this on Sam's ferry for me? If that ol' slimebag has his poster there already, put mine on top of his, okay?"

I laughed. "Okay, Dad." Folding it up, I put it in the front pocket of my overalls. I bit my lip. "Don't worry about the election, Dad. I think the best man—I mean *person*—will win."

Dad raised his eyebrows. "What do you mean by 'person'?"

I reached into my pocket, running my finger across the embossed fish on my pocket watch. "You know, the best person, that's all."

And I walked into school, wishing I'd had the guts to tell him.

Eleven

"Did your daddy give you a huggy-wuggy this morning?" one of the guys teased at lunch. I ignored him.

"Oh, Daddy! I love you!" another one said. I ignored him, too.

I opened my lunch pail and took out a chunk of cheese, a piece of corn bread, a lemon tart, and two pieces of ham.

Otis sat next to me, pulling out two boiled eggs, a slice of bread and butter, a handful of prunes, and a pork chop. "Wanna trade?"

I examined his loot. "I'll take your prunes."

"For your tart?"

"My tart? No way! How about my cheese?"

"Cheese for delicious sweet prunes from my grandpa's plum orchard? You must think I have 'Fool' written on my forehead. How about half of my prunes for your tart?"

"How about half of my tart for all your prunes?"

"Deal."

I broke my lemon tart in two and gave him the smaller half. He tried to keep one of his prunes, but I took them all. Half a lemon tart was worth way more than a handful of prunes even if they did come from his grandpa's orchard.

"Don't look now, but here comes Birdine."

I looked. Otis was right.

"I said not to look!"

"But when you say not to look, that only makes me *want* to look."

"Shhh."

"Hi, boys."

We didn't answer, pretending to be too busy stuffing our faces.

"Can I sit here?" She pointed to the desk next to mine.

We didn't answer.

"Gee, if I didn't know any better, I'd think you two were trying to avoid me." Birdine sat down and opened her lunch pail, taking out a pear, a couple of barbecued ribs, and a bowl of bread pudding.

"Wanna trade?" Otis asked, eyeing her pudding.

She looked his lunch over. "No, thanks. I don't make trades with boys who peek into library windows."

Otis dropped his pork chop on the floor. "Wh-what?"

I spewed ham all over my desk. "What did you say?"

"You heard me." She looked at both of us. "I know you two were outside the library last night."

"Me?" I pointed to myself.

"Me?" Otis pointed to himself. "Why would we want to look into the library?"

She crossed her arms. "You were both trying to find out what was going on. Just admit it."

We weren't about to admit anything.

"Funny, I could have sworn that I heard Sparky whining last night, too."

I stuffed my whole chunk of cheese into my mouth. That was one way of avoiding confrontation. My mouth was so full I could barely chew, but I got it all down with a swig of water. "Oh, I know why you heard Sparky," I said, trying to sound convincing. "I took her on a walk last night."

"By the library?"

"Um, yeah. I think we might have walked by there."

"Did you happen to bring a ladder with you?"

That Birdine. Why did she have to go and ask so many nosy questions? And why did she have to be so pretty? "A ladder? Why would I bring a ladder on a walk with my dog? Birdine, are you feeling all right?"

"I certainly am." She took a bite of her barbecued rib, smearing sauce on her nose. It looked kinda cute, all mixed in with those freckles of hers.

Otis and I didn't say anything. We just kept on eating and trying to look innocent. But I had a feeling we weren't doing a very good job of it. I had a lump in my throat. My hands were all clammy. And Otis kept tapping his fingers on his desk as if they were four tiny racehorses. We were dead giveaways. We might as well have confessed.

"Well, I guess I better move back to my desk since you two aren't talking. Before I go, I should tell you that I told my mother what I saw last night."

I swallowed hard. "You—you did?"

"Uh-huh."

"Um, what *did* you see last night?"

"I saw a boy looking in the second-floor window, watching us."

"What boy?" Otis asked, his fingers racing across the finish line.

"Well, I'm not absolutely positive, but I think it was you!"

I sighed. Maybe I was home free.

"I didn't see you, Corn, but I heard Sparky."

I looked down at my desk. *Drat that freckle-faced girl.*

"Well, bye-bye, boys."

I let out a deep breath. So did Otis.

"She's on to us," I said.

"Yeah," Otis agreed. "Like a chicken on a june bug."

"Like a coon dog on coons."

"Hey, like mold on cheese!"

We both laughed.

Otis picked up his pork chop from the floor and wiped it on his sleeve. "Wanna trade?"

I rolled my eyes.

"You know," Otis said, "one thing in our favor, she's not absolutely positive it was us. You heard her. She can't prove anything. Right?"

I shrugged. "You think her mom will tell our moms?"

"Probably. That's what moms do, you know. They tell each other everything, even the stuff we wish they'd mind their own business about."

Otis was right. Somehow our mothers always knew about our mischief almost as soon as it happened. Like the time Otis and I ran Birdine's bloomers up the flagpole. I swear, no one saw us. But as soon as I walked in the door, my mom nailed me.

Then there was the time we double-dog-dared each other and clipped about four clotheslines. Somehow our mothers knew it was us, too. *Gee, how's a boy supposed to get away with anything in this town? Now I'll have to fess up to Mom. I'd rather eat Otis's pork chop than do that.*

Twelve

Friday morning I was up and dressed when Mom came into my room.

"How's my boy?"

"Fine."

Mom sat on the edge of my bed, looking a little nervous. She fidgeted with the blue gingham trim on my bedspread. She traced the squares on my quilt with her finger. She cleared her throat. "Corn? There's something I need to talk to you about."

I swallowed hard and bit my lip. *Oh no. Did Birdine's mom tell her?* I tried to look innocent and act normal, but it wasn't easy.

"A little birdie told me that you and Otis were peeking in the window of the library the other night. Is that true?"

Drat that redheaded birdie. "Well, um. You see, Mom . . . I was, um, walking Sparky."

"And you stopped to look in the second-floor window of the library?" She eyed me. "Really, Corn. I wish you had come to me and discussed it, instead of sneaking around like that."

"Sneaking around?" I sat down next to Mom. "I'm not the only one sneaking around, you know. It looks to me like you and your *sisters* are doing a pretty good job of it yourselves." There. I had said it and I might as well finish. "Why don't you just come out and tell Dad that you're running against him for mayor? That's the right thing to do, you know."

Mom looked surprised and hurt. She stood up and walked around the room as if in deep thought. She crossed her arms and uncrossed them. "Corn? I'd like to tell your father what's going on, but I can't."

"Why not?"

"Because it's not that easy." She sat back down on the bed. "If I tell your father, he'll probably tell all the other men in town, and then they'll try to stop us. The women have to keep it quiet or our vision for the future of Umatilla will fall by the wayside."

I looked out the window. *Their vision for the future?* "Mo-om. I don't get it. If you have a vision for the future, why don't you just let the men handle it?"

"Because the men don't share our vision," she stated emphatically. "They want things left the way they are. But we women, my sister suffragists and I, see change as an integral part of Umatilla's future. We think Umatilla *needs* change if it's going to flourish."

I thought about the things Mom and her sisters wanted changed, and I had to admit that most of their ideas were pretty sensible. But she still needed to tell Dad.

Mom looked me in the eye. Her lips tightened and her nose got that pointy look it always got when she was upset. "I can't tell him, Corn. I've thought about it. Really, I have. But if I tell, I risk ruining everything my sisters and I have worked so hard to accomplish."

"But you should tell Dad."

She shook her head. "I can't. I'd like to, and I feel really bad about it."

"Do you?"

"Of course I feel bad," she said, crossing her arms again. "Don't you realize I've been lying awake each night worrying about this? It's all I think about as I'm cooking and cleaning and caring for Daisy. I'm worried sick that your father is going to take this personally."

"Take it personally? How else is he supposed to take it? Everything's personal, Mom. Even politics."

She paced the room. "When your father married me, he knew what type of woman I was. He knew he wasn't marrying someone who would just sit back and say 'Yes, dear,' and 'Anything you say, dear.' He knew how I felt about women's right to vote. If it weren't for me, your father wouldn't even *be* in politics. I'm the one who wanted him to run for mayor. I'm the one who wrote his campaign speeches. If it weren't for me, your father would still be turning train engines at the roundhouse."

I gulped. Mom was right.

"Not everyone is cut out for politics, Corn. Politics is a calling, like being a teacher or a doctor, and believe me, I don't think your father is meant for it."

"Then what did you want him to be mayor for?"

Mom tapped her finger on her lips, thinking. "I was the one who really wanted to be mayor, not Dad. And I didn't realize that until he was elected."

I thought about that for a good long time, and I knew Mom was right again. But there was something in me, way deep inside, that couldn't admit Mom would make a better mayor than Dad. And I felt like a rat.

"I keep praying I'm making the right decision, Corn. And so far I feel confident. I totally believe I'm the best person for this job."

I looked down at the floor. "What about Mr. Lanier?"

Mom laughed. "Oh, really, Corn. He doesn't give a hoot about politics. He's just in it to get even with your dad."

I nodded.

"Are you going to tell Dad?" Mom asked.

I shrugged.

Mom put her arm around my shoulder. "If you feel you need to tell him, I'll understand."

I blinked back a tear. "If I tell Dad, I'll feel like a dirty dishrag 'cause I've let you down. But if I don't tell Dad, I'll still feel like a dirty dishrag 'cause I let *him* down. Either way, I'm a low-down, dirty dishrag!"

"No you're not." Mom pulled me closer to her. "I'm so sorry you're caught in the middle of this. I wish there was something I could do."

"There is something you can do."

"What?"

I cleared my throat. "Well, you could tell me who the little birdie was who told you about Otis and me."

"Sorry, I can't tell."

"Was it a redheaded bird with freckles all over her face?"

Mom smiled and raised one eyebrow. "Never saw a bird with freckles before."

"I have. It's Birdine Bain the pain."

Thirteen

After a breakfast of scrambled eggs and fried ham, I walked into the living room, where Sparky was lying in her box by the fireplace. I scratched behind her ears and rubbed her cottony eyebrows. “How’s my Dirl?”

Sparky sniffed my hands.

Dad came walking through in his coat and hat. His hat had fuzzy flaps hanging down over his ears.

“Where you goin’?” I asked.

“I’m speaking to a group of old folks today. I’ve got to assure them I’m *not* going to double their taxes, as one dirty dog *said* I would even though he knows the mayor can’t raise taxes.” He wrapped a scarf around his neck, the lopsided pink-and-yellow one Aunt Lola had crocheted for him last Christmas—the one he hated with a passion but wore anyway, because if he didn’t Mom would get on him, reminding him how long Aunt Lola had worked on it, saying it would hurt her feelings if he didn’t wear it once in a while.

I smiled. Poor Dad. There he was, wearing that awful pink scarf with yellow stripes, trying to salvage his position. I wasn’t sure the fuzzy earflaps would help much, either.

"Can you drop me off at school?"

He looked at the clock in the hall. "Sorry, Tiger. Got to run or I'll be late." He held up the end of Aunt Lola's lopsided scarf and waved it at me.

Poor Dad. He looked pitiful.

He rubbed his knuckles over the top of my head, stepped out the door, then came back in. "Hey, I almost forgot to show you this." He tossed the morning newspaper at me. "Take a look at the front page!" The door closed and a gust of cold air whipped inside, tinkling our chandelier.

Mom walked in with Daisy on her hip. "Did he leave already?"

"Yeah."

Mom peeked out the window. "Did he wear Aunt Lola's scarf?"

I made a wrinkled-up, half-dead face.

"Good. Aunt Lola will be at that meeting and I wanted her to see him wearing it."

"But why? Then she'll think he likes it and she'll make him matching mittens for *this* Christmas."

"Oh dear. I hadn't thought of that." Mom and I cracked up. Daisy laughed, too, only she had no idea what was so funny.

"You think that's funny, Daisy Maisy girl? You want Dad to wear pink-and-yellow mittens?"

She held out her hands to me and said, "Coo-Coo!"

"Not Coo-Coo," I said. "It's Corn! Say Corn?"

"Coo-Coo!"

•

I met Otis at Elmer's tombstone.

"Did you know my shoe is nine and one-half inches long?"

I laughed. "No, I didn't know that. But take a look at this." And I pulled out the newspaper that Dad had handed me earlier.

Otis grabbed the paper and read it aloud.

"WEDDING TURNS STICKY

"December 1, 1916—What started out as a dream wedding in the home of Mr. and Mrs. Billy Crittenden of Boardman turned out to be a nightmare when an uninvited guest, who had claimed to be a relative, vanished with many of the lovely gifts intended for the happy couple.

"The groom, Donald Coleman, said he noticed a tall man in a long muskrat coat. 'He said his name was Uncle Bob, and I thought he was from my wife's side of the family. She thought he was from mine!'

" 'He took my sterling silverware service for eight!' cried the bride, Debbie Coleman. 'My crystal goblets, my china tea set, even my dish towels, they're all gone!'

"This makes the twelfth town hit in the last eight months by Sticky Fingers Fred, the most notorious pickpocket in the West. It appears this sneaky scoundrel, who turns dreams into nightmares, is working his way from west to east, preying upon large gatherings of people.

"Citizens of Oregon are urged to be alert and are encouraged to postpone all public events, especially events that have been announced in newspapers, flyers, or posters that may be seen by this criminal and used to calculate his next heist.

"There is now a reward of $600.00 for anyone with information leading to his capture. Police say he may be armed and dangerous."

"What kind of nut would want to steal dumb ol' dish towels?" said Otis. "That's pretty low. Why, I'd like to catch this creep. I'd like to rip his head off. I'd like to—"

"I'd like to ask him why he took the cuff links off a dead man," I said.

"Yeah, me too! You think he'll come to our election day parade?"

"Who knows. It's in the newspaper, so he's probably found out about it."

We walked along in the cold, making our way to school and kicking tumbleweeds.

•

After school, our quiet home was invaded by Mom's sister suffragists, carrying purses, scarves, gloves—and brooms.

They all said their greetings, then hurried into the kitchen, leaving me alone with my thoughts. *Should I eavesdrop again? No, I shouldn't. Look what happened last time. But how can I not listen with all those ladies talking about the election? They might say something I need to know.*

I tiptoed across the dining room and peeked through the cracked kitchen door. Maybe I would watch for just a few tiny minutes.

"Does Frank suspect anything yet?" pretty Miss McKee asked.

"I hope not," Mom said. She sounded worried. "Corn knows, though."

The ladies gasped.

"Otis knows, too," Mrs. Gill said. "I'm not sure how much he knows, but I found out he was looking through the library window during our meeting the other night."

The ladies gasped again.

"You think he'll tell?" asked Mrs. Burris. Little nose-picking Johnny wasn't with her today. Lucky for me. That way I didn't have to worry about offending him or some other dumb thing like that.

"He better not tell!" Mrs. Gill said. "I threatened him with his life. What about you, Flora? Do you think Corn will tell Frank?"

"I hope not," Mom said. "On the one hand, I'm mad that he found out about us. But on the other, now that he knows, I feel so bad that he's stuck in the middle, between Frank and me. Poor kid, that's a terrible position to be in."

I felt bad about it, too, and still wished she'd tell Dad. But I knew she couldn't. The other ladies were depending on her. If she told Dad, he might tell all the husbands, and who knew what they would do.

Through the crack I could just see the kitchen table. It was set with Mom's best china, the blue cups and saucers that had tiny yellow daisies on them. In the middle of the table was a red vase filled with sprigs of holly and a plate of sandwiches cut into tiny triangles. Mom was pouring tea. "So what's the latest news with our march?"

"Let's see, now," Aunt Lola said, biting into one of the triangles. She got out a clipboard and flipped through some notes. "The parade starts at the grade school, proceeds down Main, turns at Mahoney's, passes the Edwards Building, then ends at the Butter Creek Telephone Company . . . We're going to be marching behind the tractors, just as in the last election day parade. How many ladies have agreed to join our march?"

"At last count we have twenty-two," said Mrs. Smith.

"Oh, that reminds me. I ran into Canda Rattray at Wurster's yesterday," said Otis's mother. "Did you know they have pork chops on sale for twenty cents a pound? They're a little fatty, mind you, but well worth the price. Anyway, Canda said she'll march with us. And her three daughters will, too."

"Good," Mom said, smiling.

Mom passed around the plate of sandwiches. "Let's see now. That makes twenty-six. How many did we have in our last march?"

Aunt Lola flipped through her notes. "Nineteen."

They ate and talked awhile and then got real quiet.

"You think we can pull this off?" Mrs. Burris asked

Mom. "You know it's not too late to back out. We don't have to go through with it if you don't want to."

"Don't want to?" Mom's lips tightened and her nose got that pointy look. "Sisters, I've never wanted anything more in my life. If I don't do this, I'll never forgive myself. I'll always wonder what would have happened if we had only tried."

I swallowed hard. Mom was a go-getter. She'd always told me to stand up for what I believed in. And in a way, I was kinda proud. I mean, how many moms in the United States would have the guts to run for mayor? And how many would run against their very own husbands? Mom was one in a million. But then again, so was Dad.

"What will we do if Corn and Otis spill the beans?" Miss McKee asked.

"What *can* we do?" Mom said. "If the men find out, they'll surely try to stop us, but we just can't let that happen. We've got to push forward, no matter what."

"Sisters," Otis's mom said, "even if Corn and Otis *do* tell, even if every man in Umatilla finds out, we could still win this election, since we have more women than men in this town."

"Only if every woman votes for us. We can't count on that. Women have always voted for men. We have to spread the word," said Mom, "to let each woman in

Umatilla know she has a choice. She can vote for women who will work for our future, or she can vote for men who are satisfied with things just as they are. She can drag her hem through chicken droppings on dark streets for the rest of her life—or vote for us."

I bit my lip and ran up to my room before anybody found me out.

Fourteen

Sunday morning, before church started, Otis and I were minding our own business, sitting in the back pew where all the guys hung out, when who should come along and stir up trouble but Birdine Bain.

"Hi, boys," she said, sitting down in our pew. She was all dressed up in a pretty green dress with matching ribbons in her hair. *Drat that girl. Why does she have to go and be so pretty?*

I looked at Otis, and he looked at me. We decided to ignore her and picked up hymnals, pretending to be reading them.

Birdine crossed her arms and tapped her foot.

"Look, guys. I told my mother what I saw at the library. That's all."

"What'd you go and do that for?" I asked, turning a page. "You didn't have to tell."

"I did, too, have to tell," she said, turning my hymnal right side up. "I thought our mothers should know their secret was out. It's only fair."

"Then maybe I should tell my dad. That's only fair, too, you know."

"Just because I told doesn't mean you should."

"And why not?"

"Because if you tell your dad, he and all the other men will try to stop the women."

Piano music started softly, signaling that the service was about to begin and that everyone should sit down and be quiet. People sat all around us and we were trapped, right there with Birdine Bain, for the rest of the service.

"We will now stand and sing hymn number 205," said the song leader.

Everyone stood and thumbed through their hymnals. I held mine in front of my face.

Birdine whispered, "Don't you remember?"

"Remember what?"

"What Miss McKee said. About the dogs and the

cats. And how the dogs had a right to make decisions, too, you know?"

I knew. And it made perfect sense the way Miss McKee had explained it. But in an election, didn't the candidate always know who he was up against? My dad had no idea that he was competing with my mom! Besides, he was my dad, and men were supposed to stick together. I eyed Otis, looking for support, but he kept his head down in his hymnal.

"You got your essay on the Great War done?" Birdine asked as we turned to hymn number 37.

"Almost."

"Me too," Birdine said. "How about you, Otis?"

Otis looked down at his shoes. "Well, I haven't really started yet."

"You haven't? You better get going. It's due tomorrow."

"I know."

She put her hand on my arm. "Corn? How much do you have left to do on yours?"

"Just the bibliography."

"Want some help?"

I looked at Otis, then back at Birdine. "Um, no, thanks."

"Well, if you need any help, just give me a phone call."

“All right.” But I knew there was no way I’d call Birdine. Just the thought of us talking on the phone, to each other, made me as nervous as a walleye in shallow water.

•

Later that night, I couldn’t resist and went into the kitchen to use the phone. “Hello, Birdine?”

“Yes?”

“This is me, Corn.”

“Oh, hi! I can’t believe you’re phoning.”

“Me, neither. I mean, I *can* believe it, ’cause here I am, but I *can’t* believe it, ’cause I never thought I would!”

She didn’t answer.

Oh brother! This phone call wasn’t going very well. I took a deep breath. “Um, Birdine?”

“Yeah?”

“I do need some help with my bibliography.” There, I said it, even though it was a big fat lie. I didn’t need any help on my bibliography. I had gotten it all done that afternoon after church. I just kinda wanted to hear her voice.

“Do you want to come to my house? Or do you want me to help you on the phone?”

I looked down at my cozy old pajamas, the ones with little ducks all over them and a stain on the pant leg. "Um, I don't think I should come to your house right now. It's kinda late. You better just help me on the phone."

"Okay." She tried to explain bibliographies, but I didn't listen very well.

I said "Uh-huh" when I could fit it in and "Yeah" once or twice, and asked a couple of questions. When she finished talking, an awful silence filled the phone and I wasn't sure how to break it.

The clock over the mantel chimed nine-thirty. I could hear Birdine breathing.

"So," Birdine finally said, but she didn't say anything else.

I wished I could think of something to say, something to let her know I kinda halfway liked her. "Birdine?"

"Yeah?"

I bit my lip. All the words I had practiced vanished into thin air. Gone forever.

"Did you say something?" she asked.

"Yeah. Birdine? I, uh . . . I think you have pretty greenish-brown eyes."

"I do?"

"Yeah," I said. "They're the same color as seaweed."

"Seaweed?"

Did I say that?

"You think my eyes look like *seaweed*?"

Oh no! I did! "Well . . . um, pretty seaweed."

She hesitated. "Gee, thanks. I guess."

"You're welcome," I said. *You're welcome?* This conversation was only getting worse. I pounded my forehead on the kitchen wall. *Thunk. Thunk. Thunk.*

"What's that noise?"

"What noise? I don't hear any noise."

"Hmm. It stopped. Oh well, I guess I'll see you tomorrow. Bye."

"Bye!" I hung up. *Seaweed? Seaweed? How could I say a stupid thing like seaweed?*

Fifteen

Monday morning, the smells of coffee and bacon filled my nose, making me run downstairs.

At the breakfast table, Daisy was pounding her tray and smearing cottage cheese on her head.

"Hey, Daisy Maisy girl!" The only clean spot I could find on her was her ear, so I gave it a quick kiss.

"Coo-Coo!"

"Corn. Corn. Say Corn."

Daisy smiled and wiped cottage cheese on my face.

"Oh brother!"

Mom and Dad laughed.

Dad watched me fill my plate.

"What?" I asked, knowing something was up. I could tell by the way he was watching me.

"I think we should go fishing after school today."

"Today?" I almost choked on my toast. "What brought this about?"

"Oh, I've just been thinking. Lanier's got me all worked up over this election and I need some time away. You want to go?"

"Of course!" I got out of my chair and gave him a huge hug. "I'll get my gear ready and put it in the auto."

"Wait a minute, Tiger." Dad made me sit back down. "You eat. I've already got the auto packed."

"Did you get my float? The yellow-striped one? And both my poles?"

He nodded.

Daisy flipped a curd of cottage cheese onto my plate.

"Hey, Daisy! Watch what you're doin'."

She must have liked the look on my face because she did it again.

I flicked the curds right back at her. One landed on her forehead, one on her shoulder.

"That's enough," Mom said, getting out her dishrag. "No food fights."

"But—"

"No buts," Dad said.

Then another curd came flying from Daisy's tray. This time it hit Dad, and I laughed myself silly.

•

"Did you call Birdine last night?"

I elbowed Otis. "Are you kidding?"

"No. Did you phone her?"

I bit my lip. "Now, why would I want to do a thing like that? She's—she's—she's a girl."

"No fooling. Did you call her?"

I rubbed my hands together and blew into them.

"So did you?"

"Kinda."

"Kinda? You either did or didn't. Which is it?"

"Okay, okay, I did. There. Are you happy now?"

Otis smiled. "I knew you would." He kicked up

some leaves at me. Then, next thing I knew, we were both kicking leaves all over the place.

"Otis? Can I tell you something?"

"Sure."

"No, I mean really."

"Really." Otis stopped kicking and looked at me. "I won't tell, promise."

"Cross your heart, hope to die?"

"Stick a needle in my eye."

"Well, I, um . . . I kinda like Birdine."

"I know."

"You do? How?"

"You get all jittery when she's around."

Gee, I didn't realize it showed so much. "Well, that's what I wanted to talk to you about."

Otis sat down on Elmer's tombstone and got out his measuring tape. "Okay, I'm all ears. Hey, that reminds me." He measured his ear. "Hmm. Two and a half inches."

I cleared my throat. "Well, um, pretty girls make me nervous. I get all loopy and my brain goes blank, and before I know it, my knees turn weak and my words come out all stupid-sounding." I let out a big breath.

"Just do what I do."

"What?"

"I picture all pretty girls with boogers hanging out their noses."

I jerked my head back. "You do?"

"Yup."

"You do not!"

"Do too."

I scratched my chin. "Why would you want to do a thing like that?"

"Because then they seem more normal. You know?"

"Let me get this straight. You picture pretty girls with boogers hanging out their noses because then they seem more *normal*?"

"Yeah. Normal people have boogers. Right?"

"Right."

"So pretty girls have to pick their noses just like everybody else. When you see a pretty girl, just think boogers. Hundreds of boogers. Thousands of boogers."

"Hundreds? Thousands? Why not just a few?"

Otis rolled his eyes as if he were trying to teach me the ABCs, something I should already have known. He tapped me with his tape measure. "Because a pretty girl with just a few boogers hanging out her nose is still kinda pretty and still hard to talk to. But a pretty girl with a thousand, maybe a million boogers isn't near as pretty and a heck of a lot easier to talk to."

I nodded. In his own strange way, Otis made sense.

Sixteen

I emptied my lunch pail—an apple, a slice of sausage, crackers and cheese, and—oh no!—a liverwurst sandwich. Liverwurst was the most disgusting sandwich in the world, even worse than cow tongue, and that was pretty bad.

Otis pulled out a gloppy egg salad sandwich, a chicken leg, a green apple with a bite out of it, a couple of prunes, and a marble. "Wanna trade?" He eyed my lunch. "I'll give you this marble for your apple."

"You've already got an apple."

"Yeah, but I took a bite out of it and it's sour."

"I don't want your marble." I moved my apple out of his reach. "How about my liverwurst sandwich for your chicken leg?"

"Hmmm. How about my sandwich?"

"Deal." I had just made the trade of the century. Egg salad for liverwurst. I watched him take a bite, because that was our rule—once you took a bite out of something, you couldn't give it back. Yes! I was home free! "Tell me, do you really like liverwurst?"

"It's okay." He watched me take a bite of his sandwich, then he smiled.

"What?" I asked.

"My dad made that sandwich."

"So?"

"I saw him drop the egg on the floor as he was making it."

I stopped chewing.

"So if you find any hairs in it, or anything crunchy, that's why."

Birdine walked over and sat down. We both watched as she emptied her lunch pail—two doughnuts sprinkled with powdered sugar, a bruised banana, and a meat-loaf sandwich with ketchup. "Wanna trade?" she asked, but she wasn't looking at Otis, only at me.

"I, uh—" I glanced at Otis. He was pointing to his nose, then to the back of Birdine's head. He mouthed the word "Boogers."

"Well?"

It was hard concentrating on her question with Otis pointing back and forth between his nose and Birdine's head. "Um, what was the question?"

"Do you wanna trade?" She looked at me oddly.

Otis was going crazy, pointing back and forth. I tried not to look at him. "Um, let's see. How about my egg salad sandwich for one of your doughnuts?" There. Maybe trades of the century had re-trade value.

Birdine looked at the sandwich and sniffed. "What makes you think I want a sandwich with a bite out of it?"

I shrugged.

"How about your crackers and cheese for my doughnut?" she asked.

"Deal," I said. That was better than nothing. And as I took the doughnut, I noticed that her hand touched mine and stayed there a little longer than it had to. Our eyes met.

Otis tapped his nose. "Boogers," he mouthed. "Boogers."

Birdine turned around. "Is there something wrong with your nose, Otis?"

"My nose? Noooo. My nose is just fine. How's your nose?"

She looked at him, then at me. "Is he okay?"

"Oh, don't mind him," I said. "He's just got boogers on the brain!"

•

Mr. McGrath collected our five-paragraph essays on the Great War. "Class, what did you think of this assignment?" he asked.

All the kids nodded. If they said what they really thought, that five whole paragraphs was way too long, they'd get Mr. McGrath's lecture about how it wasn't anything compared to what we'd have to write in high school—five-*page* essays.

Some of the guys groaned, and I could tell they'd rather have a tooth pulled than write an essay, but it didn't bother me. I kinda hoped Mr. McGrath would assign another one, but I didn't dare tell anyone that, especially the guys.

Mr. McGrath went over the results of last Thursday's spelling test. We hadn't done too well. No one knew how to spell *Epicurus*, a Greek philosopher we had been studying, and only two people, including me, knew the meaning of *impedimenta*, the supplies or baggage carried along by an army, which often impeded its progress.

"I want you to use all your spelling words in a story," Mr. McGrath said. "Underline your spelling words and turn it in tomorrow."

Everyone moaned. But not me. I liked writing stories with my spelling words. It was fun to see what I could come up with. And sometimes, when I wrote a really good story, Mr. McGrath would let me read it out loud. That always made me feel nervous, standing up in front of the class, but afterward, at recess, kids would compliment me and say they wished they could write stories the way I did.

Otis raised his hand. "But we don't have school tomorrow, remember?"

"Ahh, yes," Mr. McGrath said, snapping his fingers. He erased *Tuesday* from the blackboard and wrote *Wednesday.*

Everyone looked relieved, and I noticed Otis smiling extra big at a girl in the back of the room. Her name was Ann. She was pretty and all, with a long ponytail, but not nearly as pretty as Birdine. She didn't have a single freckle, which kinda made her face look empty. At that moment I remembered Otis having a note in his pocket last week. *Hmm. Maybe she's the mysterious girl with pretty cursive. I'll have to engage in some investigation. Investigation* was one of our spelling words. I had that one down pat.

When school let out, Mr. McGrath stood at the door, handing out last week's graded homework and patting backs. "Good job," he told almost everyone. Then, to me, he said, "Corn, the story you wrote with last week's spelling words was exceptional. Have you ever thought about being a writer when you grow up?"

I smiled, embarrassed, loving the attention and that there were still seven people behind me in line, who I hoped heard his every word. "Well," I said, casually glancing back at the seven, "I've thought about it. But I'm a man of the water, always have been. I think I want to be a ferry operator when I grow up."

Mr. McGrath nodded in agreement. "Well, you know Mark Twain was a riverboat man, himself."

"You're right. That's how he got his pseudonym. *Mark twain* was the term used by the leadsman at the bow of a steamboat to signal that they were in only twelve feet of water." It felt good to teach Mr. McGrath something, but I was sure he already knew that. "Samuel Clemens was Mark Twain's real name."

"I see you've been studying on your own. Good job." He patted my shoulder. "You never know, Cornelius. You could be a ferry operator *and* a writer. Just keep that in mind."

"I will." I took my homework, glancing back again to see who was listening. Shucks. No one was paying any attention to me.

As I stepped outside, walking on air, Dad tooted the horn of our auto. I hopped inside, excited.

"So, how was your day?" Dad asked. "Learn anything new?"

I told him about Mr. McGrath's compliments and

how we had to write another story with our spelling words. And how I and only one other person in class knew what *impedimenta* meant.

"Corn, I'm proud of you."

"You are?"

"Sure I am. You're a good student and a good son and one heck of a fisherman!" He ran his knuckles across the top of my head.

"Thanks, Dad."

Seventeen

Our auto rambled along as Dad and I headed toward our favorite fishing spot—Chinaman's Hole, near the mouth of the Umatilla River.

There was lots of speculation as to how Chinaman's Hole had gotten its name. Sam said it was just a hole that the Chinese men had fished in, but I liked Mr. McGrath's idea better. He said it was probably where the Chinese men panned for gold and stored their boats during the gold rush. They'd wait until the wee hours of the morning, then sneak out from their underground tunnels, fill their boats, and send them downriver for the ore to be smelted without the white men knowing so they wouldn't intercept the boats and steal the gold.

I thought about the Chinese men sneaking around like that and I didn't blame them one bit. Why should they have to live with the stupid sundown law? They had every right to live the way the white men did. Then I thought about Mom and her sisters: they were kinda like those Chinese men.

We unloaded our poles, can of worms, thermos, tackle boxes, and old torn fishing quilt with squares made out of flour sacks, and walked over to the fishing dock, putting down our things.

Dad blew into his hands. "Pretty chilly out here."

"Yeah," I agreed, "but it's never too cold to fish!"

Dad's eyes met mine; he was smiling.

I hooked a worm onto my line and cast it out, watching the current carry my float downstream.

Dad tossed out his line.

"Dad?" I cleared my throat. "Um, how come you never whistle anymore? I miss that."

Dad sat real quiet for a minute. "Oh, I don't know, Corn. Guess I just have a lot on my mind. You wanna whistle? Go ahead."

I didn't want to whistle by myself, but I started in

on one of our favorite songs, hoping he'd join me, and he did.

We whistled for a while, reeling in and casting out, keeping our eyes on our floats, and it reminded me of the old days, back before Dad had become mayor.

In the distance a dog barked. A train let out steam. And the sound of the roaring river was entrancing.

"Corn?"

"Yeah?"

"I need to talk to you about something."

Oh no! He knows about Mom. And he wants to know why I haven't told him. "You do?"

He cleared his throat and looked real serious. He paused as if he were searching through his mental dictionary for just the right words. "As you know, tomorrow is election day and—"

"Wait, Dad. I can explain."

"Hold on now, Tiger. What I'm wanting to say is, would you like to be the one to blow the bugle to commence the parade?"

"The bugle? The bugle?" I let out a big breath. "Is this what you wanted to talk about?"

"Sure. Sheriff Vinson chose your name from his hat. You're the lucky winner!"

"Gee, I'd be proud to blow the bugle. Any boy would." I yanked in my line. Something had stolen my bait. I hooked on another worm and cast it back out.

"So," Dad said, pulling in his line and checking his bait. It was gone. "What was it you said you could explain?"

"Explain? Um, me?"

"You said you could explain something. What?"

I bit my lip and took a deep breath. If I had any backbone, I'd come right out and tell him. But at that very moment, I felt like a spineless jellyfish. Oh, why couldn't I just tell him? Why couldn't I just blurt out *Mom is running against you for mayor*. But I couldn't. "Um . . . Explain. Explain. Oh, I know. I was wanting *you* to explain about your plan to catch Sticky Fingers Fred. That's what I meant."

"Well, as I said, I'm posting two men at the entrances to town. They're to be on the lookout for anything or anyone suspicious."

"Do you really think he'll show up?"

Dad rubbed his chin. "Don't know. But it's better to be safe than sorry."

"Hey! I've got one! Feels like a steelhead!"

"Reel him in!"

I kept a tight line so he wouldn't throw the hook and slowly reeled him in, enjoying the fight. Back and forth he swam, and when he jumped out of the water,

I could tell he was a big one. I pulled him up on the dock, flipping and flopping. "Would you look at this?"

Dad got the stringer ready. "Looks like a keeper. What do you think, two pounds? Maybe three?"

"Yeah. Maybe even three and a half." I put my thumb into the steelhead's mouth, trying to pull out the hook. After two tries, I got it out with my worm still intact. "Say, we need Otis here. He could measure this fish for us."

Dad laughed. "Oh brother! Is he still carrying that measuring tape around?"

I rolled my eyes and shook my head. "He probably sleeps with it every night."

I hooked the stringer through the steelhead's mouth and out its gill. I dropped the fish slowly into the river and tied the stringer to the leg of the dock. The fish tried to swim away, but didn't get very far. I tossed my line back out, glad I didn't have to bait up again. It was kinda fun to see how many fish I could catch with the same worm. Once I caught three—pretty good fishing.

We sat there, our legs dangling off the dock, watching our lines and drinking coffee from our thermos. I wasn't much of a coffee drinker, but being that the only time I was allowed to drink coffee was when Dad and I went fishing, I took advantage of the moment. If Dad fixed it with lots of milk and sugar, it was kinda good.

Overhead the sky was gray, and the air smelled clean. I loved this place. But I didn't love what I was doing to Dad and I felt guilty. "Um, Dad?"

"Yes, son?"

"How's the election coming?"

"Good. I think I've got that ol' mudslinger beat, but I won't know for sure until tomorrow." He yanked in his line and hooked on another worm.

"So, are you glad that women can vote now?"

Dad cast out his line and took another swig of coffee. "Sure. They've fought long and hard. I think women in every state should be allowed to vote."

"Really?"

Dad nodded. "Women should be able to decide who they want to run their government. It's the democratic way, you know."

I'd heard that word a lot lately. "Um, do you think that women should be able to run for office, too?"

Dad smiled. "Now, that's a different story. You see, if women ran for office, I don't think very many men would vote for them, so they'd have a hard time winning."

Obviously, Dad couldn't imagine that if women outnumbered men and every woman voted for the female candidate, it wouldn't be hard at all. But maybe he had something else in mind.

"Why do you think men wouldn't vote for women?" I asked.

Dad looked real thoughtful. "Well, you see, only a few years ago women weren't even allowed to vote. So going from that to a woman holding office is a big change for men. Most men feel that women belong in the home and not in politics. It's the way it's always been."

"But just because it's always been that way doesn't make it right, does it?"

"I suppose not."

A salmon boat went by, and we waved at the fishermen. They gave us a thumbs-up, which meant they had a good catch.

"What about you, Dad?" I pretended to scratch an itch. "Do you think holding office is a man's job?"

"Well, Clara Cynthia Munson was elected mayor over in Warrenton a few years ago. And we had a woman who served as acting governor while Governor Chamberlain went to Washington for a few days back in 1909. But in general women don't hold office, Corn."

I bit my lip. "So . . . do you think a woman could, for example, become mayor of Umatilla?"

Dad smirked. "Umatilla? I doubt it. Most folks in this town are old-fashioned. They're used to being governed by a man and don't even think about a woman doing the governing. Yup, I'd say cows will fly before a woman becomes mayor of Umatilla."

I laughed. "Hey, Dad, remember that rhyme Grandpa used to say about cows flying?"

Dad nodded, smiling, and we both chanted,

"Birdie, birdie in the sky
Why'd you do that in my eye?
I'm a good boy, I won't cry
I'm just glad that cows don't fly!"

I looked up above me. Yessiree, I was glad that cows didn't fly, but I had a feeling that might be about to change.

Eighteen

That night I tossed and turned, my thoughts flipping like pancakes on a griddle.

Who would be the better mayor? Mom or Dad? Mom might be, because she's so meticulous. She always gets the job done and she always does it well. Yeah, I think Mom's the one who should be mayor.

But Dad is already mayor. He may not always get the job done and he may not always do it right, but at least he's got experience, and that's got to count for something. And he's a man and that counts for more . . . Yeah, I think Dad should be mayor.

I punched my pillow. I yanked my sheets. *I should have told Dad. I had the perfect chance.* I sighed and turned over on my stomach, my side, my back. I gave my pillow another punch. The clock chimed two in the morning, three, and I still hadn't slept a wink.

A slice of Mom's homemade bread slathered with Aunt Lola's peach preserves. That's what I needed.

I stepped into my slippers, put on my flannel robe, and padded down the stairs, trying not to make any noise. Silently I made my way to the kitchen. The door creaked open, and to my surprise, there sat Mom with white cold cream all over her face.

"What are you doing up?" she whispered.

"That's just what I was wondering about you," I said, sitting down and yawning. "I was going to get a slice of bread with preserves."

"Me too," Mom said, pointing to an open jar. "Help yourself."

I cut a piece of bread and topped it with two spoonfuls of peach preserves. I eyed Mom.

She eyed me, too, then took a sip of coffee. "What's on your mind?" she asked.

Her question made me mad. This whole eating at three o'clock in the morning business was all her fault. I gave her a mean glare. "You know what's on my mind."

"Did you tell your father anything?"

"No, but I wanted to." I licked my fingers.

Mom sighed. "Well, I'm glad you didn't say anything, Corn."

I put down my bread and stared at Mom's white face. "You know, I felt like a spineless jellyfish out there today because I didn't have the guts to tell him."

She started to put her arm on my shoulder, but I jerked back so she couldn't. It felt good to show her I was mad. So I went ahead and let her have it. "I don't like being in the middle between you two."

"I know, Corn. I'm sorry. Believe me, if there was any other way—"

"There is. Tell him. Go in there, right now. Wake him up and tell him. He's got a right to know, Mom." My face felt hot.

"I can't."

I looked her in the eye. "Is it worth it, Mom? Is it really worth it?"

"It's the future I'm thinking about, Corn."

"Maybe you need to think more about now than about the future, Mom, because there's no telling what Dad will do if you get elected. And do you know how bad I'm going to feel if he asks me if I knew and why I didn't tell him?"

Mom stared into her cup. Her face looked as if it might drip into her coffee, but it didn't.

"And what if he gets really, really mad? I mean, what if he forbids you to be mayor or something?"

"Forbids?" Mom sat up straight and started wiping her face with a dishrag. "He can't forbid me to be mayor. He's not my boss, Corn."

I took another bite of bread. I was so tired and so angry I didn't even feel like talking. If Mom was like other moms, the kind who stayed home and took care of their house and kids, we wouldn't be in this mess. But no—Mom had to be different. She had to run for mayor, and not only *that*, she had to run against her very own husband. I let out a huffy breath.

"You know," I said, pointing my finger at her, "I wish you could just stay home and be my mom. That's all I want. A mom."

"But, honey, I'll still be your mom. It doesn't matter what else I do, being your mom will always come first. Look at your father—he's still your dad, isn't he?"

"Yeah, but he's not near as good a dad since he became mayor. What if that happens to you? What if you stop cooking breakfast and stay gone too long, and what about Daisy? Who will take care of her?"

"I've already arranged that, Corn. You needn't worry. Aunt Lola said she'd be glad to help out as much as possible."

"I wish you'd just forget the whole thing and vote for Dad tomorrow." The clock chimed three-thirty. "I mean, today."

"Corn?"

I pretended to be busy eating, but I watched her out of the corner of my eye. She didn't look half bad once she got all the white stuff off her face.

"Corn, I know you're upset and I don't blame you. My mother never ran for anything, except after all seven of us kids. Day and night she cooked and cleaned and ironed. She never had the privilege of voting, and she never even thought about it because it wasn't an option."

"It's still not in most of the United States, Mom. So why do you have to go and run for mayor?"

Her lips tightened and her nose got that pointy look.

"I have to run for mayor for you and Daisy and our future. I have to run for mayor for my mother. I have to run for mayor because I believe I can do a better job than Kim Lanier or your father, and because I want men to see that limiting someone because of sex is wrong. I have to run for mayor because it just might pave the way for a woman to run for President of the United States of America one day. And you never know, Corn, that woman could be your daughter or granddaughter."

And with that, she got up from the table and walked out of the room, leaving me sitting alone in the dark kitchen, finally getting it: Mom was right—women *were* entitled to the opportunity to run for office. I didn't have to choose which of my parents should be mayor. I only had to decide whether I was going to prevent one from having the same chance to compete that the other one had. That wasn't so hard.

Maybe I could sleep now.

Nineteen

"Corn? Are you ready? We've got to leave in ten minutes!" Mom called up the stairs, bright and early on election morning.

I fastened the buttons on my Sunday suspenders. They were dark blue and matched my navy pants and socks. I looked in the mirror. "What do you think, Dirl? Do I look okay?"

Sparky perked up an ear.

I gave her a quick rubdown and kissed her nose. She tried to lick my face and got my lips all wet. "Ugh, Dirl!"

I bounded downstairs, hearing Sparky's toenails clicking on each step behind me.

Bacon popped in the skillet, and water whistled in the kettle. Mom was pinning on her hat in the kitchen mirror; Dad was standing right next to her, saying, "Thank you, ladies and gentlemen," and striking different poses.

"How's this look, Corn?" He held in his stomach and turned sideways.

I stared at him. "What are you doing?"

"I'm practicing my acceptance speech," he replied, watching himself in the mirror. "And so it is with great gratitude . . . Flora honey? Should I say *great* gratitude or *much* gratitude?"

"Either is fine, Frank."

"And so it is with great gratitude that I accept another term in office as mayor of this fine city." He held his hands out palms up as though testing for rain.

Mom's eyes met mine. She smiled and cupped my elbow. "Are you okay?"

"Yeah."

"Did you get any sleep?"

"Not much."

"Me neither." She made a face. "Go brush your hair—it looks like an unmade bed. Here, take Daisy. I've got to finish getting ready." She shoved Daisy into my arms.

Daisy smiled and hugged me. I put her down on the floor, and she followed me to the bathroom, where I gave my hair a brushing. It didn't do much good, though. My hair had a mind of its own, and today it wasn't listening.

In a matter of minutes, Mom had seen to it that we were all fed, brightly polished, and packed into our auto. Dad had decorated it with red ribbons and flags. On both back windows were posters that said: SANWICK FOR MAYOR—THE WISE CHOICE.

We stopped at Aunt Lola's house, and Dad tooted the horn.

Aunt Lola stepped out, all gussied up in her green cashmere coat, looking grand as a Christmas tree. A yellow ribbon was draped from her left shoulder to her right hip. It said: EQUAL RIGHTS FOR WOMEN. Mom wore the same ribbon.

Aunt Lola hobbled down the steps and handed me her broom. I put it on the floor of the car, next to Mom's, then scooted over to make more room.

"What're the brooms for?" Dad asked.

"We're marching with them," Aunt Lola replied.

Dad gave Aunt Lola and Mom a funny look. Then off we headed toward Main Street.

"Flora? Do I look okay in this suit?" Dad asked. He had on his brown pin-striped suit with a navy tie.

"Frank, don't worry. You look just fine. Now, how about me? Does this dress make me look like a pear?"

I snickered in the backseat and looked at Aunt Lola. Mom always worried that her figure resembled a pear—big at the bottom and small at the top.

"Flora, you look beautiful. Absolutely divine. And when I give my acceptance speech today, I want you by my side so everyone can see what a beautiful wife I have."

"Thank you, Frank." Mom turned around in her seat and winked at Aunt Lola. Aunt Lola winked back.

I pretended not to notice all the winking. I swallowed hard and kept my mouth shut.

"You know, Flora, I think you should vote for Mr. Massie for treasurer," Dad said. "He's good with money."

Mom jerked her head back as if someone had

poked her with a needle. "Mr. Massie? That penny-pinching ol' geezer who refuses to fix the sidewalk in front of Butter Creek Telephone Company? You must be joking."

"Now, Flora. You can't judge a man by his side-walk—"

"I most certainly can, Frank." She raised Daisy to her shoulder. Aunt Lola pushed Daisy's nose and said, "Beep-beep!"

"Watch out for her," I warned Aunt Lola. "Don't let that innocent face of hers fool you. She's a hair-pullin' machine."

Aunt Lola laughed and gave Daisy another beep-beep. "Is that what you are? A hair-pulling machine?"

Daisy smiled and clapped her hands. "Bee-bee."

"You seem to think that sidewalk repair isn't important," Mom said. "But it is. In fact, Frank, there are lots of important things that haven't been taken care of lately, and the ladies of Umatilla are tired of it. So don't you tell me whom to vote for. I'll vote as I please."

Now it was Dad's turn to jerk his head. "What? What are you talking about, Flora honey?"

"Don't you Flora honey me, Frankfurter. I've got a mind of my own, and I plan to use it."

Dad looked at Mom and shrugged. "Gee, I didn't mean to get your dander up. I was only trying to help."

"I know you meant well, but you don't have to tell me whom to vote for."

We rode the rest of the way in icy silence. Mom slid to her side of the seat and didn't look at Dad. Dad put both hands on the steering wheel and didn't look at Mom.

When we reached Main Street, we saw autos, horses, and wagons everywhere. There were so many people I almost felt dizzy. Dad drove around the block a couple of times, trying to get our auto in line with the other ones that were driving in the parade. Finally he found his spot. "I just love this," he said, turning around to Aunt Lola and me. "Parades make you forget all your troubles. Everyone's happy. Everyone's smiling and waving. Yes sir, I love parades."

No one said anything. Not even Daisy. She had fallen asleep on Mom's shoulder and was drooling down Mom's coat sleeve. I took a deep breath. Normally, I loved parades, too. But today was anything but normal. My heart was pounding. Would Mom win? Would Dad? I almost hoped Mr. Lanier would win.

"We'll find you two after the parade," Mom said, opening her door. "Aunt Lola and I are meeting up with the sisters for our march."

I handed Mom and Aunt Lola their brooms, then got the baby carriage out of the back for Mom. She laid Daisy down and covered her with a blanket. Daisy didn't even wake up.

"Frank?" Mom said, bending down and looking in the window.

"Yeah?"

"Good luck," she said. Then, in a lower voice, she said, "Whether you win or lose, you're still my Frankfurter, and I love you."

Dad looked surprised. "Well, thank you. I love you, too."

Then Mom and Aunt Lola disappeared into the crowd, pushing Daisy's carriage and carrying their brooms.

Dad looked at his wristwatch. "Corn, you've got about forty-five minutes before the parade starts. You got your pocket watch?"

I took it out and opened it. "Yup. It's nine-fifteen."

"Good. Sheriff Vinson's counting on you to blow the bugle at exactly ten."

"Okay, Dad." I stood there a minute, not sure what to say. "Um, Dad?"

"What, son?"

I looked at him and bit my lip. "Good luck, Dad." I shook his hand.

"Thanks, Tiger. I'll make you proud of me today."

"I'm always proud of you, Dad. Win or lose, you're the best dad a boy could have." And I really meant it, too.

•

The street was lined with people. Everywhere I looked, I saw men, women, kids, dogs, and of course chickens. Wagons and autos were parked helter-skelter. Streets were blocked off with ropes. Vendors lined up their pushcarts on the board sidewalks.

"Hot dogs! Get your hot dogs!" a man shouted. He wore a funny hat that looked like a huge hot dog. People were gathered around him, holding out their nickels.

"Peanuts! Fresh-roasted peanuts!" another called. "Two cents a bag!"

"Lemonade! Sweet as sugar!"

Children were laughing and running and playing tag. Dogs were barking and chasing chickens. Babies were crying on their mothers' shoulders. And fathers were talking in groups, smoking cigars, and admiring one another's horses.

"Hey, Corn!"

"Hey, Sam!"

"Woo-wee!" Sam said, shaking my hand and looking my Sunday coat up and down. Little Johnny was at his side. "Don't you look dandy! Ready for the big election today?"

"Oh yeah! I'm ready," I said, thinking *if only he knew*. I looked at little Johnny. As usual, his finger was up his nose. "Johnny? Your finger's gonna get stuck up there."

Johnny wrinkled his nose and stomped on my foot.

"Ouch!"

"Now, Johnny," Sam said, "tell Corn you're sorry."

Johnny didn't say anything. Instead, he stuck out his tongue.

I wasn't about to let that bratty little nose-picker get the best of me, so I stuck my finger up *my* nose. "You know, this feels pretty good. You ought to try it, Sam."

Sam looked at me oddly. "Ooooh, I get it." He put his finger in his nose. "Hey, you're right. This *does* feel good. I think I'll keep it here all day long."

"Yeah," I agreed, eyeing Johnny. "Me too."

Johnny looked at me. "You really gonna?"

"Sure," I said, hoping nobody I knew was walking by, especially one of the guys or Birdine. Last thing I wanted was for any of them to see this.

"Are you gonna, Daddy?"

"Yeah," Sam said, winking at me. He poked his middle finger in his other nostril. "This is fun."

I cracked up. Good ol' Sam, always joking.

Johnny stood there, staring at Sam. Finally he said, "Stop it. You look dumb, Daddy."

"I'll tell you what," Sam said. "I'll make a deal with you. I'll stop—if you'll stop."

Johnny thought about that a good long time. "Okay, Daddy." And just like that, he pulled out his finger.

Sam raised his eyebrows in disbelief. A smile spread across his face. He started to give me a hand shake, but since his fingers had been up his nose, I guess he decided against it. Which was pretty good thinking, since that's where mine had been, too. So he just nodded his chin at me. "Thanks, Corn."

"Anytime," I said. And they went to find Mrs. Burris.

Twenty

"Corn! Corn! Over here!" Otis waved at me from the hot dog line.

"Hi! How's it going?"

Otis shook his head. "I'm starting to grow a beard, if that tells you anything."

I laughed and stood in line with him, telling him about what had just happened with little Johnny and Sam.

"Oh no!" Otis said, pretending to look serious. He covered his heart and made his voice sound like a woman's. "I hope you didn't hurt his delicate feelings!"

"Heaven forbid!" I said.

At last we made it to the front of the line, and we both walked away with hot dogs covered in mustard, ketchup, relish, and a mountain of onions.

"Now we're going to have onion breath," I told Otis, blowing in his face.

"Oh no. That's enough to kill a horse."

"I better stay away from Tip and Nip, then."

"Yeah and you better not kiss Birdine, either."

I thumped him on the head. "What makes you think I want to kiss Birdine?"

"Come on, Corncob. It's written all over your face."

"It is?"

"Yup."

"Well, how about you, Oatmeal?" I teased. "I saw you smiling extra big at Ann in the back of the classroom yesterday. Is she the one who wrote you that note in real pretty cursive the other day?"

"Maybe."

"So what's up with you two?"

"Nothing."

"Then why's your face turning red?"

"It's not."

"Is too."

"Oh, be quiet."

"Oatmeal? If I tell you something, will you promise not to tell?"

"Cross my heart, hope to die," Otis said.

"Stick a needle in your eye?"

He nodded.

"An extra long needle that's really sharp?"

He nodded again.

"Well"—I got up real close so no one else could hear—"I've never kissed a girl before."

Otis rolled his eyes. "Course not. Neither have I. And we better not kiss any today. Halitosis. That's one of our spelling words. Remember?"

I remembered. As we walked along, an old man in

a blue coat and a brown hat bumped into us, or maybe we bumped into him—I wasn't sure. Something about him looked familiar. He had a long white beard, kinda like Santa Claus, and walked with a cane.

"Hey, watch it," he grumbled.

"Oh, I'm sorry," I said.

Otis and I hung around on the corner, watching pretty girls go by and daring each other to whistle at them. Otis whistled at one girl, then ducked down, so it looked as if I was the one who'd whistled. Then I got him back, only I whistled at an old lady, which made Otis mad. After a few whistles, though, we couldn't do it anymore because we were laughing too hard.

"Say," Otis said. "I ran into Sheriff Vinson earlier. Aren't you supposed to blow the bugle at ten?"

I reached down into my pocket for my pocket watch, but it wasn't there. I searched my other pocket. It wasn't there, either. I pulled my pockets inside out. No watch. "Oh no! I've lost it! My grandpa's watch! How am I going to blow the bugle when I don't know what time it is?"

"Let's retrace our steps," Otis suggested. "It's got to be here somewhere."

We walked back to the pushcart and the man with the huge hot dog hat, keeping our eyes on the ground.

There were so many people, though, so many long skirts dragging, I didn't know how we'd ever find it.

"Excuse me, sir?" I asked, butting in line. "Have you seen a gold pocket watch?"

"No, son, I haven't." The man handed a lady three hot dogs, one with mustard, two with ketchup. "But if you want to know what time it is . . ." He dug down into his pants pocket. "It's—it's—" He got a funny look on his face, then dug into his other pocket. "Hmm." He searched his coat pocket. "Sorry, son. I guess I'm not much help. I must have forgotten my watch today."

We walked back to the street corner where I had talked to Sam and little Johnny, finding nothing but footprints, chicken droppings, and a button.

"Otis? I have a funny feeling . . . Remember that grumpy ol' man we bumped into?"

"Yeah."

"The one with the long white beard?"

"Yeah."

"I don't think we bumped into him. I think he bumped into us."

Otis scratched his head. "What are you talking about?"

"I'm talking about Sticky Fingers Fred. I think that was him. I think he took my pocket watch."

"But why would a pickpocket want to mess with *your* pocket? You're just a kid."

"Yeah, but the hot dog man isn't. And his watch is missing, too."

Otis looked as if he had just remembered something important. He put his hand into his left pocket, but it came up empty. His face turned white. "Oh no!"

"What?"

"My spring-loaded, nickel-plated tape measure—it's gone!"

"Let's go tell Sheriff Vinson." We took off, looking for the sheriff. "Do you remember what that old guy was wearing?"

"I think he had on a blue coat. Yeah, it was blue. And a brown fedora hat."

"And a cane," I added.

"Corn! Corn!" Sheriff Vinson shouted, waving his arms. "It's ten o'clock! Where have you been?" He shoved the bugle into my hand.

"He's here! He's here!" I said.

"Who's here?" Sheriff Vinson asked.

"Sticky Fingers Fred!"

"That's impossible. We've got men posted at both entrances to town!"

"I'm tellin' you, he's here. He bumped into us and took my pocket watch and Otis's tape measure, and the man with the hot dog on his head can't find *his* pocket watch, either!"

"The man with the hot dog on his head?" Sheriff Vinson looked at me as if I wasn't making any sense.

"I couldn't find my pocket watch and Otis thought maybe I lost it in the hot dog line, so we asked the man with a hot dog on his head if he had seen it and he said no but that he'd tell us what time it was, and when he looked for his pocket watch, it was missing, too!"

"And my tape measure is gone!" Otis added.

"Are you sure about this?"

We both pulled out our pockets. "See? No holes!"

"Boys, we don't want to cause a panic. Corn, I want you to blow this bugle so the parade can begin."

"But—"

"We'll need to carry on as if nothing is wrong. Then, while the parade is going, we'll be on the lookout."

I took the bugle and gave it my best shot. I'd never blown a bugle before, so it came out sounding like a sick moose. All the people on the sidelines clapped and cheered. Some of the guys from school whooped and hollered.

Immediately, the Pride of Umatilla Marching Band started marching down the street—shiny shoes, polished buttons, crisp uniforms—clanging cymbals and banging drums to the tune of "Yankee Doodle Dandy."

Sheriff Vinson put his hands on my shoulders. "Now tell me what this old fella who bumped into you looked like."

We described him as best we could.

"I want you two to calm down and act normal. And keep a lookout."

"But what if we see him?"

"Try not to let him out of your sight. Get an adult to help you. And remember, he may be armed and dangerous."

"Don't worry," Otis told Sheriff Vinson. "If he's here, we'll find him. Isn't that right, Corn?"

"Right."

Twenty-one

The Little Miss Walleye Princess waved from the back of a wagon, followed by the Junior Miss Walleye Princess, who was none other than Ann, the girl with the pretty cursive who sat in the back of our classroom.

"Look!" I pointed. "There's your girlfriend!"

Otis folded down my finger. "She's not my girlfriend." Then he smiled extra big and waved wildly.

The fancy horses were next, trotting in two lines, their manes and tails braided with ribbons. Then came the clowns and the decorated bicycles. Then the autos, their drivers tossing candy to all the kids on the sidelines.

"Sanwick for mayor!" Dad shouted, throwing peppermints and licorice sticks. "Sanwick for mayor! The wise choice!"

"Dad! Dad!" I ran to the window of our Model T.

"Son, get back!" He handed me some licorice. "You're not supposed to be in the street!"

"Dad! Your hunch was right! Sticky Fingers—he's here—he took my pocket watch!"

"And my tape measure!" Otis added.

Dad hit the brakes. "He's here? What's he look like?"

Otis and I described the old man who had bumped into us.

Dad slapped his steering wheel and shook his head. "Boys, I'll keep an eye out as I'm driving. You two watch for him. If you see him, get Sheriff Vinson."

We pushed our way through the crowd of kids running after candy and made our way to the sidewalk, but there were so many people we couldn't see over all the heads and hats.

"It's no use," Otis said. "I can't see anything. We need to be up high to get a good look."

Just then a tall tractor drove by, all decorated with flags and stars. It was pulling a flatbed trailer with two people dressed up to look like Uncle Sam and Betsy Ross. They were waving and tossing candy. Otis and I looked at each other with the same idea, then took off after the tractor and jumped onto the back of the trailer.

"Hey! What's going on?" the Uncle Sam man asked, giving us a mean glare.

"We're looking for Sticky Fingers Fred!" Otis said. "Just keep waving!"

"You mean that pickpocket?" the Betsy Ross lady asked. "The one in the newspaper? You think he's here?"

"We know he's here," I said, and quickly told them our story.

Behind us, Mom and her sisters were marching and chanting, sweeping their brooms from right to left. In front of their group, Miss McKee and Birdine held a large banner made from a twin bedsheet and painted in bright red letters: EQUAL RIGHTS FOR WOMEN!

The ladies marched on, some sweeping brooms,

some pushing baby carriages, and some, like Mom, trying to do both. On the front of Daisy's carriage was a sign that read I'M A WOMAN, TOO!

"Clean sweep! Clean sweep! This town needs a clean sweep!"

Poor old Aunt Lola was a little out of step, but trudging right along.

"Clean sweep! Clean sweep! This town needs a clean sweep!"

Otis elbowed me. "Hey! Is that him?"

I looked. There in the crowd stood a tall man in a blue coat with a brown fedora. My heart skipped a beat. But when he turned around, I saw only Mr. McGrath licking an ice cream cone.

"Clean sweep! Clean sweep! This town needs a clean sweep!"

"You look on that side of the street," Otis said, "and I'll look on this side."

We kept an eye out and rode along, waving as though we were part of the parade.

"I think that's him!" Otis whispered. He pointed to his side of the street.

A man with a long white beard and a blue coat was walking down the sidewalk. He bumped into a lady, and as he walked away, he put something into his pocket.

"That's him, all right!" I said. "Let's nab him!"

We jumped off the flatbed trailer and headed in the man's direction.

"Hey! Where'd he go?"

"There he is!"

We ran toward the blue coat, but there were so many people we lost him.

"Wait a minute!" Otis said. "How are we gonna catch him? We can't just walk up to him and say, 'You're under arrest.' He'd take off running and we'd never see him again."

I looked around. I saw the banner that Miss McKee and Birdine were carrying. "Come on. I've got an idea!"

We headed straight for the marching ladies.

"Clean sweep! Clean sweep! This town needs a clean sweep!"

I grabbed one side of their banner and Otis grabbed the other. We took off with it, much to the ladies' chagrin.

"Now where'd he go?"

We stood there a minute, trying to gather our wits. Birdine came up to us. "This isn't funny, boys! Give us back our—"

"There he is! Heading toward Butter Creek Telephone Company!" We ran as best we could, through the crowds on the sidewalk, dodging people and pushcarts, dogs and chickens, baby carriages and bicycles. When we got right behind him, my heart almost stopped. What if it wasn't him? What if it was just another man in a blue coat, like Mr. McGrath?

"Hey! What's the big idea?" he asked, turning his head. And as he did, I saw a scar going from his left eye into his long white beard. A cold shiver raced down my spine.

"Get him!" I shouted.

He tossed his cane and took off running, the fastest old man I'd ever seen.

As he got closer to the Butter Creek Telephone Company, fate was on our side, because he didn't know what we knew—that Mr. Massie was a penny-pinching ol' geezer who refused to replace the three boards missing in his sidewalk.

"Ahhh!" Sticky shouted, tripping and falling. He pulled himself up, limping, but we ran around him, wrapping him like a candy bar in the EQUAL RIGHTS FOR WOMEN banner. He fell to the ground.

"You took my pocket watch and I want it back!"

"Yeah! And I want my tape measure!"

I yanked off the fake beard.

"You're making a big mistake," he said. "Let me loose!" He got back on his feet and tried to run, but took one step and fell back down.

I stuck my hand under the layers of the banner and reached down into his coat pocket, pulling out a fistful of jewelry, watches, and coins—with Otis's tape measure and my pocket watch.

Sheriff Vinson and Dad came running. So did all the marching ladies, carrying their brooms. When they realized we'd just caught Sticky Fingers Fred, the ladies gave him the thrashing of a lifetime.

"Hey! Stop! Stop!" he shouted, trying to duck their brooms. "Help!"

"There's my pearl necklace!" said one lady, feeling her neck.

"And there's my diamond ring!" said another.

The hot dog man came running up. He took off his huge hot dog hat and began slapping Sticky's face. "Give me back my pocket watch!" he shouted.

I leaned down by Sticky's ear. "Just tell me one thing. Why'd you steal the cuff links off a dead man?"

"Because I could!" he growled.

Sheriff Vinson pulled both of Sticky's hands out from under the banner and handcuffed them behind his back. "You thought you could fool us. You thought you could get away with this, didn't you?"

"Yeah, and I would have, if it hadn't been for those two!"

Dad patted Otis and me on the back, smiling proudly. "Good going, boys! Looks like you two will be getting a hefty reward!"

Newspaper reporters squeezed in around us. "How'd you two boys catch him? What are your names?"

"Corn San—"

"That's Sanwick," Dad said, "S-a-n-w-i-c-k."

At the same time, Mr. Lanier ran up and started spelling *his* name. I had to laugh. Even in the midst of catching the most notorious pickpocket in the West, those two were at it again!

Twenty-two

After Sheriff Vinson took Sticky Fingers Fred to the clink, Dad and Mr. Lanier fought over who was going to treat Otis and me to fresh-squeezed lemonade, some hot roasted peanuts, and another hot dog smothered in onions. Seems they both won, which Otis and I didn't mind a bit.

At noon, folks began making their way to the

Castle, our new high school, to wait their turn to slip into the janitor's closet, which had been turned into a makeshift voting booth. There, among the mops and brooms and the smell of lemon floor polish, Umatilla's fate—*my* fate—was being decided. Would it be Mom? Dad? Or Mr. Lanier?

My stomach felt as if I'd swallowed a whole batch of Indian sinkers. Of course, all those onions didn't help any, either. My head ached, and my hands were cold and clammy. I could barely think straight, wondering whose name was being written on the ballot cards in that little closet.

Otis and I watched as men and women took their turns. We couldn't tell if more women had voted than men. So far, it looked even-steven. But when we counted all the people waiting to go in, there were a few more women than men. Some of the women weren't voting, though; they were just with their husbands.

That seemed odd to me. Here women had the right to vote, and some of them didn't even use it. They had a right that thousands of women wanted, that thousands of women were marching for and pushing for and even being thrown in jail for, and they acted as if it were nothing special. *Gee, when I get old enough to vote, I'm voting, no matter what.*

"So, what are you two going to do with all your reward money?" I knew that voice. It belonged to pretty Miss McKee.

"Gee, um, I hadn't thought about it," I said. "Guess I'd like to buy a split-bamboo salmon rod. I've been eyeing the one in the front window of the hardware store. It's got a hundred-yard fly reel that's light as a feather."

"How about you, Otis?"

Otis shrugged. "I've been eyeing that new fishing pole, too. Maybe we'll both get one."

"Be sure to put some up for college," Miss McKee said. "That much money would almost pay for your whole college tuition."

We nodded as she walked off into the crowd. "So," I asked, "you gonna go to college?"

"I dunno. Are you?"

I shrugged. "Mr. McGrath says I should be a writer when I grow up. But I really want to be a ferry operator."

"Why not do both? You don't have to stick to just one thing when you grow up. Look at President Lincoln. He was a storekeeper, and a lawyer, and lots and lots of other stuff."

"Yeah, that's what Mr. McGrath said about Mark Twain. How about you?" I asked.

Otis scratched his head. "I've been thinking about working on Grandpa Blythe's orchard. You know, grow plums to make prunes."

That didn't sound very appealing to me. "Why would you want to do that?"

"There's a lot of money in prunes." Otis looked real serious. "Prunes are a good business. Look at all the folks who drink prune juice."

I started to smile, but I didn't. If prunes were his idea of fun, then who was I to scorn them?

We sat around, watching people go into the Castle, then come back out. They always went in looking solemn, then came out smiling.

"I guess you didn't tell your dad," Otis said, sipping lemonade and throwing peanut shells at me.

I dodged a shell. "Nope." I threw one of mine and it hit him in the nose. I laughed.

"You think we did the right thing?" Otis asked. "I mean, by not telling?"

"Yup."

"You think our moms will go down in history books? And that kids will be reading about them a hundred years from now?"

I shrugged. "We'll find out pretty soon. The voting booth closes in about ten minutes."

Those last ten minutes were the longest ten minutes of my life.

More women came out smiling. More men came out smiling. I felt like wiping those smiles right off their faces. Didn't any of them know what I was going through? I bit my lip. I bit my fingernails. Heck, I bit everything I could get my teeth on, even the top button on my coat.

When the booth closed, folks made their way back to Main Street and hung around in front of the post office while the votes were tallied. There was an eerie silence among the women. Mom's eyes met mine, and she winked at me. I was so nervous I couldn't wink back. I couldn't do anything except sit and wonder.

Mom came over and hugged me tight. "It's okay, Corn," she said. "Whatever will be will be." She looked nervous, too, and I noticed as she walked back to her sisters that she kept wringing her hands and looking at her watch.

In a little while Dad and Mr. Lanier came walking up. They seemed to be in a trance. Their hair was disheveled, their eyes were glazed, and they were mumbling to each other.

Dad sat down on the steps of the post office and ran his hands over his bald spot.

"Dad?"

He didn't answer.

"Dad?" I waved my hand in front of his face.

He didn't even blink. "Dad? Are you okay?"

"Cows, Corn. Cows are flying."

•

". . . and so, dear friends and citizens of Umatilla, I'm happy to represent this fine city of ours and serve as your next mayor," Mom said, with Dad standing by her side. "It is with utmost respect that I take up my responsibilities, as do the other six women who have been elected today."

The crowd, which had gathered around the post office, seemed to be split down the middle. The women were clapping and cheering. The men were shaking their heads and looking just as confused as Dad and Mr. Lanier.

"It's a joke!" one man shouted. "That's what this is, isn't it? You women are playing a joke!"

Mom's lips tightened and her nose got that pointy look. "If I didn't think we could give this town the improvements it deserves, I'd be the first to step down from office. I promise you this—women or not,

Umatilla is going to have the best government it's ever had!"

Another man shouted from the crowd. "How about you, Frank? What do you think of this petticoat coup?"

Dad just stood there, his hair going in all directions. "Well . . . I, uh, I think it's a shock to all of us!" He shook his head and put his arm around Mom, then motioned to the other elected women. "All I have to say is, never underestimate the power of a woman!"

Newspaper reporters arranged their tripods, opened their camera shutters, and shouted, "Hats off, gentlemen!"

Puffs of smelly white smoke filled the air as the reporters fired their flashes, causing everyone's eyes to water.

"Oh dear," Mom said, fanning the air, "I hope my eyes were open!"

"What are you going to do now that your wife has booted you out of office?" one reporter asked Dad.

Dad lifted his shoulders. "Go back to work at the roundhouse, I guess. But now that I think about it, I'm definitely going to spend more time fishing with my son!"

"Did you hear that?" Otis asked, elbowing me.

"Yeah," I said, smiling.

"Can you step aside so I can get a photo of your wife?" another reporter asked.

Dad stepped aside and more flashes were fired.

"Can we get all the elected women together? I want a photo of the mayoress and her council."

Otis's and Birdine's moms stepped to the front of the crowd. So did Mrs. Burris, Mrs. Smith, pretty Miss McKee, and, to my surprise, Aunt Lola. They stood proudly holding their brooms and smiling.

Birdine walked up. "What do you think?"

"I think I'm prouder than a dog with two tails," I said, and I really meant it, too.

I glanced sideways at Birdine, her freckles looking like drops of sunshine. She glanced sideways at me. My knees started to weaken, but then I remembered Otis's solution and pictured her with a million boogers hanging out her nose.

"So, um, you wanna walk around?" I asked Birdine.

"Sure," she said.

"Sure," Otis said.

I gave Otis a dirty look. "I meant Birdine."

"Oh, I get it." He put his hand in his pocket and pulled out his tape measure.

When he started to walk off, Birdine grabbed his arm. "I almost forgot."

"What?"

She handed him a note. It said *To Otis* in real pretty cursive. "Ann asked me to give you this."

I nudged Otis. "Another note, eh?"

Otis smiled. "She's crazy about me."

"Then why don't you go find her?" I asked.

He shoved the note into his pocket and took off through the crowd.

"So, um, do you, well . . . would you like to kinda . . . hold hands?" There. I'd asked her. Then I remembered my onion breath. Oh no! I blew into my hand to get a good sniff.

"What are you doing?" she asked.

"Me? Oh, um, nothing." I turned my head, still sniffing. It wasn't too bad. "Got any chewing gum?"

Birdine's face turned white. She breathed into *her* hand. "Oh no! Do I have bad breath?"

"No."

"Good. I ate a hot dog covered in onions and I thought—"

"Me too!"

We both laughed. Birdine held out her hand. And just like that, I took it in mine. Her hand was as soft as I'd imagined, I had to tell her. "Um, Birdine?"

"Yeah?"

"Your hand's just like a horse's nose!"

"A *horse's nose*?"

I'd done it again! "Well, um, have you ever petted a horse's nose?"

"Yeah."

"Then you know how soft it is. And that's what I was trying to say, that your hand is soft, like that."

"Oh."

We walked along, hand in hand, listening to all the vendors' calls.

"Pretzels! Pretzels! Get your salty pretzels!"

"Taffy! Freshly pulled taffy!"

We passed a few of the guys from school, even Otis and Ann, but they were too busy eating taffy to notice.

"Wanna race to the hot dog stand?" Birdine asked. "I'm dying for another hot dog loaded with onions!"

"Me too!"

"Want a head start?" she asked.

"Me? Why would I want a head start?"

" 'Cause last one there is a rotten walleye!" And she took off running.

"Hey!" I shouted, running after her. "Do you like to fish?"

"I *love* to fish!" she called back.

•

The news about my mother spread quickly, and her photo was printed in newspapers all across the nation. Umatilla really did get the clean sweep in government that the ladies had hoped for, and Mom and her sisters quickly set out to make the changes they had planned.

Otis and I made the headlines, too. We were the envy of all the guys at school, and Mr. McGrath gave us extra credit for standing up and telling what it was like to capture a real live creepy criminal. We both ended up getting A's on our essays about the Great War. And when Mom came to class to tell what it was like being mayor, I was so proud, I thought I'd bust the buttons right off my jacket.

Dad took Mom's becoming mayor real well, even better than I had hoped. He got back his old job at the roundhouse, and now he has plenty of time for fishing. The other day we even whistled a duet in church. Dad says that whistling is a lost art and that more folks should try it.

The six-hundred-dollar reward money was split between Otis and me. We each bought new fishing poles. I got my mom a store-bought dress and a fancy new hat. I got Daisy a stuffed bear with real long hair that she could yank out all she wanted. I bought Dad a new spinner. And the rest I put in the bank, as everyone said I should.

Sticky Fingers Fred turned out to be a man named Harper D. Pitwad. According to the newspapers, he had been a migrant fruit picker who turned to a life of crime after deciding that picking pockets was more profitable then picking apples and figs. He got fifteen years in prison, and everyone was pretty happy about that.

As busy as Aunt Lola was, watching Daisy and working on the council, she still found time to crochet Dad a pair of mittens for Christmas to go with the pink-and-yellow scarf she had made last year. Poor Dad. He looked pitiful, but he smiled and acted as if it were the best gift he'd ever received. I laughed, until I saw what she had made me—a long orange scarf with green fringe.

Elmer Diffenbottom officially got laid to rest next to his kinfolks in the cemetery. Even though we had to walk a little farther, that didn't stop us boys from rubbing his tombstone for good luck. It came in handy for important events such as test taking and fish catching and girl kissing. Of course, I still didn't know much about the last, but I was on my way, thanks to Otis and his boogers.

AUTHOR'S NOTE

Operation Clean Sweep is a work of fiction, in which I have taken such liberties as making the region appear to be more heavily populated than it actually was. However, it is based on the true clean sweep in government that occurred in Umatilla, Oregon, in 1916, just four years after Oregon women had received the right to vote.

As historical journals report, the women of Umatilla were not happy with the way the men were running their city. Over a card game, they secretly decided who among them would run for which political office. They spread the word to the other women, keeping it secret from the men.

On December 5, 1916, after approximately forty Umatilla citizens stepped out of the voting booths, Mrs. Laura Stockton Starcher had proudly defeated her husband, incumbent Mayor E. E. Starcher, receiving twenty-six votes to her husband's eight.

Other women elected that day were Gladys Spinning; Anna Means; Florence Brownell; Stella Paulu, who was elected mayor in 1918; Bertha Cherry, who later became Umatilla's public librarian; and Lola Merrick.

News of Umatilla's clean sweep spread across the country. Many of the nation's leading newspapers covered the incident as though it were a joke and referred to it as a "Petticoat Coup," but the seven women took their positions seriously.

Their first order of business was to replace Umatilla's streetlights and to pay the back electric bills. Then uneven streets were graded and covered with new cinders. Sidewalks were repaired. Several graves were exhumed from the streets and moved to the cemetery.

Citywide "Cleanup Weeks" were enforced, and a team of men was hired to haul trash, with specific orders from the council to "remove the toilet from the yard" of one citizen. If anyone didn't abide by the new orders, the city performed the cleanup at the citizen's expense.

There was more. Any chicken that ran freely through the streets of Umatilla was threatened with being penned or shot and thrown into a stewpot. Public fountains were erected. A campground was built. Trees were planted on all city lots. The Columbia River Highway, which is still a major transportation conduit, was routed through the city after the women convinced the highway committee that Umatilla held the flattest land that followed the river.

The changes didn't end there. Monthly garbage service began. A library board was appointed, and a library fund was added to the city's budget. Regulations were made regarding the parking of automobiles, and numerous other laws were enacted.

Then, in 1920, only four years after Umatilla's clean sweep, their goals accomplished, the women quietly stepped down from office, letting the men once again lead their city government. What had been thought of by some as a joke turned out to be four years of the best leadership Umatilla had ever seen.

Certainly the accomplishments of these remarkable women helped pave the way for August 27, 1920, when the Nineteenth Amendment to the United States Constitution was passed, granting all women the right to vote.